'You can't r... Kate.

Some day it may just happen and you won't be able to fight it. You were unlucky. Yes, you were hurt, but you have to start trusting someone again, some time.'

She pressed a shaking hand to her mouth. 'I don't have to let it happen. I won't let it.' The words were whispered as he drew away, but she thought in sudden terror that it was already too late. She was already in love with Sam.

Jean Evans was born in Leicester and married shortly before her seventeenth birthday. She has two married daughters and several grandchildren. She gains valuable information and background for her Medical Romances™ from her husband, who is a senior nursing administrator. She now lives in Hampshire, close to the New Forest, and within easy reach of the historic city of Winchester.

Recent titles by the same author:

RULES OF ENGAGEMENT
HEART IN HIDING

A LEAP IN THE DARK

BY
JEAN EVANS

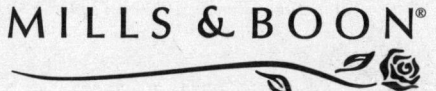

DID YOU PURCHASE THIS BOOK WITHOUT A COVER?

If you did, you should be aware it is **stolen property** as it was reported *unsold and destroyed* by a retailer. Neither the author nor the publisher has received any payment for this book.

All the characters in this book have no existence outside the imagination of the author, and have no relation whatsoever to anyone bearing the same name or names. They are not even distantly inspired by any individual known or unknown to the author, and all the incidents are pure invention.

All Rights Reserved including the right of reproduction in whole or in part in any form. This edition is published by arrangement with Harlequin Enterprises II B.V. The text of this publication or any part thereof may not be reproduced or transmitted in any form or by any means, electronic or mechanical, including photocopying, recording, storage in an information retrieval system, or otherwise, without the written permission of the publisher.

This book is sold subject to the condition that it shall not, by way of trade or otherwise, be lent, resold, hired out or otherwise circulated without the prior consent of the publisher in any form of binding or cover other than that in which it is published and without a similar condition including this condition being imposed on the subsequent purchaser.

MILLS & BOON and MILLS & BOON with the Rose Device are registered trademarks of the publisher.

*First published in Great Britain 2000
Harlequin Mills & Boon Limited,
Eton House, 18-24 Paradise Road, Richmond, Surrey TW9 1SR*

© Jean Evans 2000

ISBN 0 263 82285 0

*Set in Times Roman 10½ on 12 pt.
03-0101-50742*

*Printed and bound in Spain
by Litografia Rosés, S.A., Barcelona*

CHAPTER ONE

DR KATE DAWSON locked her car door and hurried breathlessly up the steps and into the cooler interior of the Gables Surgery.

Easing a strand of honey-blonde hair behind her ear, she paused at the reception desk and glanced at her watch.

'Hi, I'm not too late, am I? Don't tell me I've missed everything.'

Smiling, sandy-haired, Australian Tim Blake signed another letter, tucking it inside a folder before reaching across the desk for the remains of a cup of coffee. 'No chance. It's still going on. I just came out to answer the phone, then remembered I wanted to get these letters off in this evening's post.'

With a sigh of relief, Kate put her briefcase on the floor. 'Today of all days I had to get an emergency call. Phew, this heat.' She glanced anxiously in the direction of the staffroom. 'I'm going to have to go in there. I'm just not sure how I'm going to face it. I hate the thought of saying goodbye to Doug.'

Tim leaned back in his chair, wearily flexing his shoulders. 'I have to admit it's certainly not going to be the same around here without him.'

'I still can't believe it's happening.' Kate dropped a small bundle of case notes onto the desk, before easing her blouse from her clammy skin. 'Doug's a damn good doctor. He loves his job here. The sponsors have no right to put him out to pasture.'

'Oh, come on, Kate.' Tim smiled wryly. 'You know it

wasn't exactly like that. Besides, whether we like it or not, they *do* have some say. Let's face it, without them we wouldn't have any kind of medical service here on the island and we need it, badly. I'd say that gives them quite a big say in what goes on.'

'Whose side are you on?' Kate gave a slight smile. Reluctantly she had to admit that it was true. 'I just don't like the idea of having a new boss more or less foisted on us without as much as a by your leave. I mean, what do we know about this new man, Stafford...or whatever his name is?'

'Slater. Sam Slater. He seemed nice enough to me. It's a pity you were on leave when he came over for a visit. But you did get a copy of his CV. He seemed keen and he certainly has the necessary qualifications, trained at one of the best medical schools. He had some good ideas.'

'I'll bet he did!' Kate muttered ungraciously. 'So why would he be interested in coming to a small island like Hellensey?'

'Maybe he just wanted a change. People sometimes do.' A smile tugged at Tim's mouth as he rose to his feet. A tall, rangy figure, he was dressed appropriately for the September heatwave in pale trousers and a short-sleeved shirt. 'We had a bit of a chat when he came for his interview and I showed him round. He seemed to like the set-up generally and has a few ideas of his own he'd like to discuss.'

'Oh, has he indeed?' Kate found herself battling against a feeling of resentment. 'Well, we'll have to see about that.' Clearly Dr Sam Slater was going to need some watching.

'Give him a chance, Kate. He's signed a twelve-month contract.'

'And I imagine he has an option to renew.'

'That's usual, Kate. Come on, be fair.'

She sniffed hard. 'Well, I just happen to think Doug's done a lot for the people on the island, that's all. Until he set up this practice, admittedly with help from the sponsors, there were next to no medical facilities, apart from one half-day surgery a week and the small cottage hospital.'

'I do know that, Kate. I don't need convincing. But it *was* Doug's decision to go.'

'Whose side are you on, anyway?'

He grinned and put an arm round her shoulders. 'Hey, come on, this isn't like you. For Doug's sake, put your brave, smiley face on and let's go in and get it over with, shall we?'

She sighed, following reluctantly as he led the way into the crowded staffroom where Tim headed off in the direction of the remnants of a buffet lunch.

'Hi.' Jill Vaughan, the practice manager, raised her voice above the noise to greet Kate's arrival. 'We were afraid you weren't going to make it in time. Here, have a drink.' Smiling, she thrust a glass into Kate's hand. 'Here you go, strictly non-alcoholic.'

'Just as well or I might be tempted to drown my sorrows.' Kate held the cool glass briefly against her cheek. The heatwave had lasted for almost a month, leaving her skin lightly dusted with freckles and her temper frayed. She glanced round the room. 'How's it going?'

'Pretty much as you'd expect. We're all putting on a brave face.'

'Have I missed the speeches?'

'No such luck.' Sister Sue Reynolds, the petite, dark-haired practice nurse, joined them. 'I think Doug's hoping he might just be able to slip away.'

'Not much chance of that.' Jill grinned. 'I'm beginning to think half the island population has turned up to see him off.'

A slight exaggeration, but only just, Kate thought as, glass in hand, she edged her way carefully through the crowd.

At the age of sixty-two, Doug Parker was still a good-looking man, and his smile was genuinely welcoming as he reached out to clasp Kate's hand.

'Kate, my dear. I've been wondering where you were.'

'Sorry, I had to go out on a call, but I wasn't going to miss this for the world.' She kissed his cheek and with an effort managed to smile. 'Things aren't going to be the same here without you, you do know that?'

He patted her hand and chuckled. 'Some may say that's not a bad thing.'

'You know that's not true. I shall miss you. We all will, but me especially.' She gulped hard. 'You were there when I needed someone. Won't you change your mind and stay on?'

His smile faded slightly. 'Can't do that. Decision's made.' He patted her hand. 'Things will soon settle down, believe me. Besides, the practice needs someone younger, someone with more energy.' He looked at her. 'You don't need me any more, Kate. You're doing just fine.'

Which was true, she thought, at least for most of the time. There were whole days now when she didn't even think about Colin.

There was a general murmur of protest. Kate gave herself a tremulous mental shake and someone said, 'Kate's right. We were doing well with you here.'

'You're all being very kind.' Doug held up his hand. 'But the truth is that the past few years have been hard work, damned hard work. Fun, rewarding, watching the practice grow into what it now is. But I've had enough. I feel I've done my bit and it's time to bow out.' Doug's brow furrowed slightly as he looked from one serious face to another. 'All I ask is that you give the new chap a break.'

'Question is, will he give *us* a break?' Tim joked.

A ripple of laughter momentarily broke the tension.

Doug smiled and then immediately became serious again. 'Look, be fair. This job has changed since the practice was set up five years ago. There are more people living on the island. We get more tourists. I don't need to tell any of you that the demands made on the medical services have grown.'

Kate frowned. 'Tell me about it. I was called out to a burns case. That's why I was late getting here. It was a young child.' She toyed with her glass. 'He'd managed somehow to get hold of a box of matches and set his clothes alight.'

Doug's hand rested briefly over hers. 'It must have been nasty.'

'Yes, it was. I feel so sorry for the parents. You can imagine what sort of state they're in.'

Tim frowned. 'Is he going to be OK?'

'I'd say it's touch and go.'

'You sent him over to the mainland hospital?'

'I had no choice. We don't have the facilities here to cope with that degree of injury. But it will take time to get him there and I'm not happy about the delay.'

'Thank God it doesn't happen too often. But that doesn't make it any easier to deal with now. Things need to change.' Doug looked at them and gave a rueful smile. 'I'm sure they will change but Dr Slater is going to need your support. You owe him that. You owe *me* that. We've been together a long time. Don't let me down now.'

Kate swallowed hard. Jill Vaughan sniffed and fumbled in her pocket for her hanky.

'Jeez,' Tim said gruffly. 'Come on, mate. You'll have me crying in my beer if you're not careful.'

There was a tiny ripple of laughter. Taking several deep breaths, Kate said jokingly, 'All right, then, so where is he, this Mr Wonderful? I can't wait to meet him.'

'I'm glad to hear it.' The deep masculine tones came from behind her, making Kate jump, and she turned to find her stare met by a pair of cool blue eyes.

She stood, transfixed, feeling her colour deepen beneath a disturbingly intense appraisal as the coolly brooding glance of the man standing in the doorway subjected her to a flagrantly masculine appraisal and, without being aware of it, she took up a defensive stance.

Her breath caught in her throat and she swallowed thickly. She felt dwarfed, but it wasn't a physical thing. It was something far less tangible, a sense of dominant masculinity which was overpowering.

She felt as if an electric current had passed through her body. It wasn't just the overwhelming sense of self-assurance which seemed to emanate from him as he stood there, though that in itself was sufficient to send a shiver of awareness running down her spine. It was something in the piercingly blue eyes that raked her slender figure and delicate features with an intensity that almost took her breath away.

She was immediately conscious of every line of his taut, muscular body, from his shoulders beneath the open-necked shirt to a slim waist and lean thighs beneath the jeans he was wearing.

Sam Slater wasn't a day over thirty-five and aggressively masculine.

His gaze shifted to Doug. 'Sorry I'm late. I got held up.'

The two men shook hands.

'Don't worry about it.' Doug smiled. 'Most of you have

already met Dr Slater. I know you'll all quickly come to appreciate what a valuable asset he's going to be to the team.'

'Oh, God,' Kate muttered under her breath. 'Don't tell me. Superman to the rescue.'

Lucy Foster, the practice receptionist, giggled and Sam Slater's mouth tightened ominously as his gaze locked broodingly with Kate's.

'Did you say something, Dr…?' He frowned. 'Dr…?'

Kate swallowed hard. 'Dawson. Kate Dawson.' Behind him she was vaguely aware of Tim grinning as he poured a cup of coffee and handed it to Sam. 'Only that we're glad to have you join us, Dr Slater.' She found herself staring into thickly lashed, disturbingly blue eyes which at that moment were filled with a sardonic amusement that made her pulses quicken even as her own blue eyes flashed her annoyance. Her cheeks flushed.

'Good. That's what I thought you said.' His gaze went from one to the other and his mouth relaxed suddenly into a smile. 'I know this can't be easy for any of you, but I hope to be able to talk to each of you individually once I've had a chance to settle in. In the meantime, if you have any problems, my door will always be open.'

Doug smiled, cleared his throat and put his empty glass on the table. 'On which note I think I can safely bow out and leave you to it.'

'Stay in touch,' Kate said thickly, ignoring the brooding look cast in her direction as she hugged Doug. 'You take care of yourself, now, hear?'

Doug kissed her cheek. 'Go easy on him, Kate,' he said quietly. 'Give him a chance, eh?'

'Sure.' Her voice broke with emotion. 'I just think he might have given you a little more time to move out first, that's all.'

Doug patted her shoulder, waved and was gone, leaving behind him a silence which no one seemed to want to break.

Tim poured more coffee and handed round the cups. 'I gather you've spent some time abroad?'

Sam Slater spooned sugar into his cup. 'I did a couple of years or so with the VSO in Africa. Came back to England about four months ago.'

Tim whistled appreciatively. 'That must have been tough.'

'It wasn't without its challenges. But I enjoyed it, most of the time.' He laughed, a rumbling and surprisingly pleasant sound. In any other circumstances Kate might have found him attractive but right now, standing at the window, watching Doug drive away, she resented every bone in Sam Slater's physically perfect body.

'You'll probably find all of this a bit of a let down then,' she said bluntly.

'Oh, I dare say it will have its own particular challenges, too.' His steady gaze unnerved her. 'But I shall enjoy sorting them out.'

She swallowed a mouthful of too-hot coffee, feeling it burn her throat as the cup rattled into the saucer. 'Yes, well, perhaps you'd like me to show you to Doug's...*your* office. I'm sure you'll want to make yourself at home.'

'Talking of which,' he said evenly, 'I imagine we all probably have work to do.'

Sue Reynolds glanced at her watch and gave a gasp of dismay. 'Oh, lor, that can't be the time. I've got Mr Jackson coming in five minutes for his blood-pressure check.' Putting her empty cup on the table, she headed for the door. 'See you later, folks. Oh, and welcome to the Gables, Doctor.'

'Sam. The name's Sam.' He held open the door, smiling

as they all trooped out towards Reception. He spoke to Jill. 'I'd like to fix up a practice meeting fairly soon. I think we all need a chance to get to know each other and I have a few ideas I'd like to discuss. Perhaps you could fix a time that will suit everyone?'

Jill smiled. 'Certainly. I'll do that, Doctor.'

'Good. I'm sure we're all going to pull together and make a great team.' The blue gaze narrowed. 'Isn't that right, Dr Dawson?'

Kate almost choked. The man was insufferable as well as arrogant. Well, others might be easily won over by good looks and a smile, but he needn't think she was going to fall for it.

Flinging him a look of disgust, she gathered up her bag and headed for the door. 'Yes, well, I can't stand here gossiping all day. Some of us have work to do.'

'Just one moment, Doctor.'

She gasped as the door slammed to a close in front of her, barring her escape.

'I think we need to have a talk, don't you?'

'Oh, I don't think so.' She lifted a finely arched brow. 'There's really nothing to say.'

'Oh, but I think there is.' He studied her, taking in the firm set of her mouth, the truculence in the taut angle of her jaw, before he moved away to stand with his hands in his pockets. 'I've upset you.'

'Upset!' Her head jerked up and she gave a short laugh. 'You couldn't wait to step into Doug's shoes, could you? Couldn't you at least have waited until he was out of the door before you started making your presence felt?'

His dark brows drew together. 'I can understand that you might resent someone coming in to take Doug's place. I admire your loyalty, but let's get a few things straight, shall we? In the first place, I didn't drive Doug out—he chose to go.'

'Doug loved his work.'

'I'm not saying he didn't. But in spite of what you may think it *was* his choice.'

'That's easy to say.'

A muscle flicked in his jaw. 'There's something you obviously don't know. I may be at risk of betraying a confidence here but we have to work together, you and I, and I think we'll do so more amicably if we feel we can trust each other.'

'I don't understand,' Kate said tautly. 'What exactly are you trying to say?'

He looked at her and frowned. 'Doug has a heart condition.'

She felt her heart give a sudden thud as she stared at him. 'Doug? Ill! No! I don't... There must be some mistake.'

'I'm afraid not. He's going to need heart bypass surgery—fairly soon.'

She expelled a harsh breath. 'But... Why didn't he say anything? Why keep it a secret?'

'He didn't want any fuss. That's why he didn't want anyone to know until he'd gone. No one except the sponsors, of course. Obviously they had to be told.'

Kate stared at him bleakly. 'When? How long...?'

'Has he known? About six months.'

'As long as that?' She was shocked.

'I gather he hasn't been feeling well for some time. He went to see a specialist.'

Kate took a deep breath. 'That must have been when he decided to take a few days off at short notice. We all thought he'd decided to take Elizabeth over to the Lake District to see their son.' She shook her head. 'We all thought he looked tired and needed a break but... I can't believe we didn't guess.'

'You've no reason to reproach yourself.'

'Haven't I?' she asked tautly. 'Doug has been a good friend. I was still pretty wet behind the ears when I joined the practice. He didn't have to take me on.'

'No, he didn't,' he said evenly. 'And I don't believe he would have done if he'd had any doubts about your ability to do the job. Or are you saying that he was mistaken?'

He stood looking at her and for a few crazy seconds she was suddenly, disconcertingly, aware of him as a man, and a very attractive man at that. Until now she hadn't noticed the tiny lines of tiredness edging his mouth, but they were there, adding a kind of ruthlessness which momentarily left her feeling vaguely shaky.

Colour flooded her cheeks as with a start she jerked back to the realisation that he was speaking.

'I...I'm sorry?'

'I was saying that we all of us owe it to Doug to make things work, don't you think?' His eyes met hers. 'I want us to be able to work together and that will be easier if I have your support.' He frowned. 'This practice needs someone who's prepared to give one hundred per cent commitment. I promise you that for as long as I'm in charge here that's what I'll give, and I expect the same from everyone else. I don't want a fight.' His voice was grimly determined, but her own was equally so as she faced him.

'What's the matter? Afraid of losing, Dr Slater?'

He straightened up and she saw the cool amusement in his eyes. 'Oh, I never lose, Dr Dawson,' he said softly. 'But then, that's something you've yet to learn about me. In the meantime, I'd like to think that we can at least be friends.'

'Friendship has to be earned, Doctor.'

'True.' He smiled. 'Will it help if I apologise? We got off to a bad start. Maybe I could have handled things a little more sensitively. It isn't easy, stepping into someone else's shoes, especially when that someone is well liked and respected.'

Kate licked her dry lips. 'So what exactly are you suggesting?'

His mouth twisted. 'Well to start with, you could try calling me Sam. I've never gone in much for formality.'

She tested the sound and found it surprisingly pleasant. 'All right—Sam.'

Humour glinted in his eyes. 'May I take it, then, that I can count on your full co-operation?'

Her heart gave an odd little flutter. Too much coffee, she told herself sharply. 'I beg your pardon?'

The blue gaze glinted. 'Professionally speaking, of course.' He glanced at his watch. 'Yes, well, I must get on. I'll see you in the morning, bright and early.'

Without waiting to see the effect his words had, Sam turned on his heel and walked away. But not before she had seen the gleam of amusement in his eyes.

Kate's mouth tightened. Well, really! The man was too arrogant for words. It was galling to discover that her hands were actually shaking as she opened the door. This was ridiculous! She only had to work with the man, she didn't have to like him. So what was it about Sam Slater that was making her so irrationally edgy?

Breathing hard, she marched briskly through to Reception and collected her diary and briefcase, before making her way to her room.

Seated behind the desk, she took several deep breaths and turned to gaze out of the window, telling herself she wouldn't think about it. But, somehow, something told her that with Sam Slater it would never be quite that simple.

CHAPTER TWO

THREE days later it seemed that summer had vanished. Kate parked her car, climbed out and locked the door, shivering slightly as a gust of wind sent a flurry of leaves blowing across the car park.

'Sorry I'm late.' She put her briefcase on the floor in Reception. Her cheeks were flushed and she paused briefly to peer across the desk at the open diary. 'Have I missed anything?'

'I hope not. I only just got here myself.' Tim came through from the office, carrying a mug of steaming coffee. He looked tired and harassed.

Kate smiled sympathetically. 'Problems?'

'You could say that.' He kneaded at his eyes. 'I was called out at three this morning. Young Barry Saunders apparently managed to wrap his car round a tree. Somehow, don't ask me how, he climbed out and walked home where he collapsed.'

'Oh, no.'

'His parents were worried, obviously, and I can understand why. When I arrived he was liberally spattered with blood and appeared to be unconscious.'

Kate frowned. 'How bad was it?'

Tim gave a short laugh. 'Actually, apart from a couple of minor cuts and the fact that he was as drunk as a skunk, he was fine. Kept insisting the tree had moved.'

'You're joking!'

'Absolutely not.'

'Sounds fairly typical.' Lucy Foster grinned as she came through from the office with a pile of cards.

'You know him?'

'Oh, yes. We were at school together. When he deigned to turn up, that is.' She fumbled through papers on the desk in search of a pen. 'Barry's been the local tear-away for as long as I can remember.'

'Nothing's changed, then.'

She laughed. 'It doesn't sound like it.'

Stifling a yawn, Kate shrugged herself out of her jacket, hanging it on the peg. She was flipping through her diary when a tall figure walked into Reception, his arms full of crushed cardboard boxes.

He smiled. 'Good morning.'

'Good morning.' She felt oddly flustered. 'I...er, how are you settling in?'

'Fine. Or at least I will be, once I sort out the rubbish from the necessities.' He glanced around, spotted a bin and tossed the boxes into it, the flexing of his muscles disturbingly evident as he did so.

'I'm afraid the cottage is pretty small. Well...' she smiled '...Elizabeth always complained that it was.'

'It's fine for what I need.'

'You certainly haven't wasted much time getting settled.'

Blue eyes regarded her with amusement as he brushed dust from his hands. 'I figure the sooner I get sorted, the sooner I can start pulling my weight around here.'

'I expect we could have managed for a while.'

'I'm sure you could.' His mouth twisted. 'I wasn't implying any criticism. By the way—' he raised his voice slightly '—I think perhaps we'd better get started if we're going to get through this meeting before surgery starts.'

The phone rang and Jill shook her head, moving aside to make room. 'Wouldn't you just know it? Even when I arrive early I'm sure someone out there knows the second I hang up my coat.'

'I know the feeling,' Kate murmured. 'This isn't my idea of the best way to start the day. *And* I missed my cornflakes.'

'Help yourselves to coffee if you want it, everyone. Bring it through to the office and make yourselves comfortable. We've got a lot to get through and not much time.'

'So what's new?' Kate was juggling her cup and jacket and reaching for her briefcase when she stumbled. Instinctively, Sam reached out, grasping her arm to steady her.

'Here, let me.' In one easy movement he took the briefcase from her. 'Don't want any nasty accidents, do we?' His eyes glinted and Kate felt the breath catch in her throat as a feeling of physical awareness swept through her.

'Thanks.'

He inclined his head in acknowledgement. 'Any time.'

A small pulse began to hammer in her throat. She withdrew her arm from his grasp, but not before she had seen his mouth curve in silent amusement.

'Right, folks, let's make a start, shall we?' He waved them all to seats. 'I know this meeting was arranged at short notice, but it seems to me that getting together like this, perhaps once a week before surgery, will give us all an opportunity to discuss any problems we're likely to come up against.'

Tim sat up and reached for his coffee. 'So you're suggesting we make them a regular thing?'

'Yes.'

Kate met his gaze. 'Doug didn't feel regular meetings were necessary. Every now and again, yes, but—'

'Doug was under a lot of pressure,' he said evenly. 'I'm not saying we aren't—quite the contrary—but in my opinion a regular weekly get-together will give us all a chance to talk to each other and to air any small worries before they turn into large grievances or problems.'

'Sounds logical to me.' Tim helped himself to a biscuit as Jill entered the room and settled herself into a vacant chair.

'Have I missed anything?'

'I suspect we're only just getting started,' Kate murmured.

Sam looked at the small group. 'Perhaps someone would like to start the ball rolling. Kate?'

'What exactly would you like to talk about?'

'Anything you think might be relevant. For a start, I'd like to know a bit more about the set-up here on Hellensey.'

Tim looked at Kate and she nodded. 'You go ahead. You know more about this than I do.'

'Well, I suppose you know that until five years ago the only medical service available on the island was a visiting GP who came over from the mainland once a week to hold a half-day surgery, and we have a small cottage hospital.'

Sam frowned. 'Hmm. Not exactly an ideal arrangement. So what happened in the event of an emergency?'

'More or less what happens now,' Jill said. 'We shipped patients over to the mainland on the local ferry. It wasn't an ideal solution, certainly not for seriously ill patients, but we had no other choice. We simply didn't have the facilities here for dealing with anything major.'

'So when did things change?'

'About six years ago. A tourist bus went off the road and rolled down a cliff. We found out later that the driver had had a heart attack.'

Lucy nodded. 'The locals did what they could, obviously. We did what we could with the minor injuries but the rest needed the facilities of a large hospital, which we didn't have—still don't have.'

'Doug was the visiting GP at the time,' Tim put in. 'He worked wonders, but after that everyone knew things had to change.' He eased his shoulder muscles. 'Doug called a meeting of the local residents.'

Jill smiled. 'I reckon everyone on the island turned up.'

Tim nodded. 'I was over here, visiting my parents, which is why I happened to be on the scene at the time, thank God. Anyway, the upshot of it was that it was decided that, at the very least, the island must have its own full-time general practice.'

Lucy smiled. 'It sort of gained momentum from there.'

'Doug roped in the sponsors,' Tim said. 'Don't ask me how. He just seemed to have a remarkable talent for that sort of thing. There was no way we could have raised the necessary cash on the island. Anyway, they asked him to head the health centre in return for regular funding and the promise of a high-speed ferry link between the island and the mainland.'

'And you were recruited,' Sam said.

Tim laughed. 'Like I said, Doug could be very persuasive. Not that it was a difficult decision to make. I'd been working in a practice on the mainland. I wasn't particularly happy with the inner-city environment so it was no hardship to move back here.'

'And you?'

Kate felt a faint rush of colour invade her cheeks as Sam's gaze swept over her, taking in the classic lines of her straight, knee-length skirt and the soft, bronze-coloured silk shirt.

She shrugged. 'As Tim said, Doug could be very persuasive. I answered an advertisement for a GP to work on the island. I was…I was looking for a change of direction and it seemed to offer what I needed.' She gave a wry smile. 'I came to Hellensey intending to do three months locum work. Doug talked me into staying.'

'I take it you have no regrets?'

'Absolutely none. Doug was the best. A good friend, a good doctor, great to work for.'

'That's quite an act to follow.'

Kate looked up sharply, expecting to see a cynical smile on his face, and was surprised to find that he was perfectly serious. She frowned. 'He'll be missed, not only here but by everyone on the island.'

'I don't doubt it. So...' Sam rose to his feet, dug his hands in his pockets and went to stand at the window 'what we all need to know is where we go from here. There must be questions you'd like to ask me?'

'You said you thought certain things need changing.' Tim put his cup on the table. 'What exactly did you have in mind?'

Sam's dark brows drew together. 'I understand that the practice doesn't carry out any minor ops. I wondered why?'

Kate flicked him a look. 'Basically, it's down to lack of time and funds.'

Lucy frowned. 'What sort of changes did you have in mind?'

'Nothing too drastic. Removal of cysts, moles. Some suturing. That sort of thing.'

'You do realise that minor surgery doesn't attract a fee?' Jill put in.

Sam nodded. 'But I think that needs to be weighed against the benefits to patients.'

'Not to mention the extra work involved.' Sue Reynolds, the practice nurse frowned.

'That, too, of course.' Sam smiled. 'But at the moment, as I see it, if we refer a patient to a hospital surgical department on the mainland, he has to wait, what...three months for an appointment?'

Kate gave a slight laugh. 'In an ideal world—if we're lucky.'

He nodded. 'And then another six months before the minor surgery can be carried out?' His mouth twisted. 'Not good enough, is it?'

She had to agree that it wasn't. In fact, she had broached the subject discreetly on more than one occasion with Doug, but he had been against it, mainly, she suspected, because of the cost of funding the enterprise.

At the same time she resented the implication behind the softly spoken words. 'I hope you're not suggesting, Doctor, that we've been doing less than our best?'

'I'm not suggesting that.' Sam looked down at her from where he stood by the window. 'What I *am* saying is that, with a little reorganisation and co-operation, we can do things to improve the service we offer to our patients.'

There was a brief silence during which they looked at each other.

Tim shifted uncomfortably in his seat. 'I can't honestly say I enjoyed performing surgery myself. Not even minor ops.'

'I don't see that as a problem,' Sam said evenly. 'It isn't necessary for all of us to take on the commitment. From the brief study I've made of the figures so far I'd anticipate we could handle, say, one or two minor surgeries a month. Emergency cases as and when, obviously.'

He'd obviously done his homework, Kate thought. She drained her coffee and put her cup on the table. 'So whoever happens to be here at the time gets it, you mean?'

'More or less. Do you have a problem with that?' The blue gaze was vaguely disconcerting.

'No, I don't think so. If we can give a better deal for the

people in our care then we have a responsibility to do so. I'm all for it.'

'Good girl.'

The genuine note of pleasure in his voice sent a tiny and thoroughly illogical frisson of happiness running through her, and she felt the faint tide of colour swim into her face as she sent him an answering smile.

'As I said, it's for the patients.'

A faint smile twisted the corners of Sam's mouth. 'Well, at least that's one problem solved. What's next?'

Jill said, 'Books.'

'Books?'

She nodded. 'Or, rather, lack of.'

'Hear! Hear!' Sue added her own voice to the conversation. 'The practice library consists of a few fairly tatty medical journals, and most of those are out of date. We need books for general reference, especially if you're serious about taking on minor ops.'

'I'll go along with that,' Tim said. 'Ideas change, treatments change.'

Sam looked from one to the other. 'OK, so what do you suggest?'

Jill raised an eyebrow. 'Bearing in mind, I take it, that the budget is stretched just as far as it will go and you can't guarantee that the sponsors will come up with extra funds?'

Sam frowned. 'It might be worth an approach to the drug companies to see if they might be willing to donate books, or maybe even contribute to a practice fund.'

Kate laughed. 'You really think they'll agree?'

'It worked at the last practice I was with. Most of the companies are only too happy to stay on friendly terms with GPs.' Sam nodded. 'Yes, I reckon it's worth a try.'

'Well, if you want to dictate a few letters, I'll whiz them

into the post today.' Jill made a note on her pad, before looking at each of them in turn. 'Anything else?'

'There is just one more point I'd like to make.' Sam returned to his seat.

Kate smiled sweetly. 'Only one? Surely not.'

'For now.' Blue eyes glinted. 'I'd like to reorganise the patients' record-card system.'

Kate laughed aloud. 'You're not serious?'

'Perfectly serious.'

Tim looked at him. 'Have you any idea of the amount of work that will involve?'

'I think so.' Sam frowned. 'In the first place, I think we can get rid of a lot of excessive paperwork.'

'Well, I'll certainly go along with that.'

Sam grinned—like a Cheshire cat, Kate thought uncharitably—very attractive, very smooth Cheshire cat.

'What I'm suggesting is that each patient's record is sorted for any major diagnosis or chronic drug therapy. We evolve a system, a chronic disease register.'

Kate frowned. 'You mean things like diabetes, heart disease?'

'Hypertension, asthma. I can think of a few others.'

'And then what? I mean, I take it there's some purpose behind the exercise?'

A smile tugged at his mouth. 'In spite of what you may think, I'm not just looking to make work.'

'I'm glad to hear it.' Jill stretched, easing the muscles in her back. 'You might just have had a mutiny on your hands.'

'Seriously, I think the practice could benefit enormously by having patient information readily to hand at the flick of a switch. It means, for instance, that we'll be able to follow up diabetics, screen them for eye disease, that sort of thing.'

Tim frowned. 'It would certainly be useful to have an instant retrieval system of all patients due for cervical or breast screening.'

'So, you think it's worth considering?' Sam looked at each of them in turn.

Tim nodded. 'Sounds reasonable to me.'

'I think I'd find it useful for following up patients who are on a particular treatment regime,' Sue said.

Jill looked less convinced. 'Have you taken into consideration the cost of this exercise? Not to mention the time involved in sorting and computerising all this information.'

'I know it isn't going to be cheap. I've spoken, briefly, to the sponsors and they agree that in the longer term the new system will pay for itself. As for the extra administration work, yes, I agree, it's going to be time-consuming. Which means that we may need to think about taking on some extra help.'

Kate sighed and briefly closed her eyes. There was something about Sam Slater that reminded her of an irresistible force. He'd scarcely been at The Gables more than five minutes and already, somehow, she just knew that things were never going to be quite the same again.

Somewhere in the distance a phone started ringing. Lucy groaned. 'Sorry, folks, I'll have to answer that. Surgery's due to start in ten minutes.'

'Do you still need me?' Sue was also on her feet. 'Only Mr Jackson is due in at nine for his blood test.' She glanced anxiously at her fob watch. 'He's nervous enough as it is. I'd hate to keep him waiting.'

'No, that's fine. You carry on.'

Kate was on her feet, too, briskly gathering up her briefcase. The day had scarcely begun and already her head was aching.

All in all, it was a busy morning, with the usual crop of

sore throats, aching backs and one confirmed pregnancy to offer a little light relief.

Kate reached for the next card. 'Mrs Duncan.' Smiling, she waved the red-eyed forty-year-old to a chair beside her desk. 'You look decidedly uncomfortable. Tell me, what I can do for you.'

'It's this cold, Doctor.' The woman held a tissue to her nose and sniffed hard. 'It's gone on for weeks. I just can't seem to get rid of it. My eyes are sore, too. I'm really fed up with it all.'

'Yes, I'm sure you must be.' Kate frowned. 'You say it's gone on for weeks. How long precisely?'

'Well, most of the summer it seems like. I've never had anything like it before.'

'Hmm.' Kate made a careful examination, gently pressing a finger against the woman's cheek-bones and then the area between her brows. 'Is that at all painful?'

'No, well, not really.' Eileen Duncan shook her head.

'What about headaches?'

'Yes, I do seem to have had rather a lot lately.'

'And your throat—perhaps we'd better take a look. Yes, that does seem slightly inflamed.'

'I don't understand it. I never get colds. It's such a nuisance, too. I mean, I work in an office. It's almost becoming a standing joke that I never stop sneezing.'

'Yes, I can see that could be a problem.' Kate smiled sympathetically. 'Just as a matter of interest, do you have the windows open at work?'

'Well, yes, at least during this very hot spell.'

Kate nodded and smiled. 'Well, if it's any consolation, I think what you've got is hay fever.'

'Hay fever!' Eileen Duncan stared at her. 'But summer's just about over.'

'You did say it's been bothering you for some time and,

whilst it's most common during the spring and early summer, it can occur throughout the year.' Kate looked at her patient's record card. 'I see from this that you live some way out of town?'

'Yes, that's right.'

'So you're actually in the countryside?'

'Yes. We live in a cottage just down the lane from Hemming's Farm.' She looked at Kate. 'But we've been there for the past five years and this is the first time I've ever had anything like this.'

Kate smiled. 'The allergy can be caused by pollen from trees, which usually causes symptoms in spring. Or it may be grass, which causes problems in summer, but there are other causes. It can be dust mites or some animal furs.'

'But we only have the cat and he's been with us for the past nine years, so it can't be that.'

'No, I agree, it doesn't seem very likely.' Kate looked at the woman. 'I wonder, you say you live next to a farm. Has the farmer planted a different crop recently?'

Eileen frowned. 'Oh. Yes! Now that you mention it. I was talking to his wife and she did mention... Well, fancy that. I can't remember what it was.' She laughed. 'You think that may be it?'

'More than likely.' Kate smiled. 'It's possible the new crop has just come into flower, or is ready for harvesting. Anyway, I can give you something to relieve the symptoms. I'll also write you up for some anti-inflammatory eye drops, which you'll need to use several times a day, and I'll give you some antihistamine tablets. They may cause some drowsiness, in which case, if it's a problem, come back and we'll try you on something different. Obviously, you mustn't drive while you're taking the medication.'

She had just seen the last patient of the morning and was looking forward to a hurried coffee-break when someone tapped at the door and came in without waiting for her to respond.

Kate frowned. Lucy in Reception had said there were no more patients. Perhaps she had somehow managed to miss one of the cards. Her frown deepened as she looked up and saw Sam Slater. His gaze was directed, frowning, from her open briefcase to her face, and she found herself thinking that he really was quite good-looking in a rugged sort of way.

She swallowed hard. 'Did you want to see me?'

'Just a brief chat, if you can spare the time.'

'I'm still rather busy.' She made an exaggerated play of shuffling the pile of case notes, and was relieved when the telephone rang. But any hopes she might have entertained that he would simply turn and leave were doomed to disappointment. He remained, stoically gazing round the small surgery as she dealt with the patient's query.

When finally she put the phone down, Sam was standing with his hands in his pockets, staring up at a small watercolour on the wall. His stance seemed to emphasise the power in the shoulders beneath the jacket.

'It's nice.' He nodded towards the painting.

Unable to resist the temptation, she straightened the frame.

'Is it a local scene?'

'The harbour, on the far side of the island. It was painted by a local artist.'

'It's good.'

She nodded. 'I like it.' She gazed up at the painting showing small fishing boats on a grey, winter sea. She smiled slightly. 'I don't think he's been painting for long. I bought a couple of his other pictures at a sale. Not that I know anything about art.'

Sam laughed. 'Nor do I, but does that matter?'

'I suppose not.' She turned and as she did so her body brushed against his, sending a mass of ill-timed signals running through her. Startled, she glanced involuntarily up at him and drew herself up sharply. 'You said you wanted to see me. Is it urgent? I still have some house calls to make.'

'Ah.' His smile revealed even, white teeth. 'I was going to suggest that I might come with you.'

'What—*now?*'

'Just to get the lie of the land, so to speak. It would help me to find my way around the island and give me a chance to introduce myself to a few people.'

She wanted to refuse but knew that to do so would sound petty. It was bad enough having to work with the man here at the practice, without having him follow her around like some stray puppy. Not that there was anything in the least puppy-like about Sam Slater!

His blue eyes regarded her with an unreadable expression. Only the slight tremor at the corner of his mouth suggested that he had read her thoughts.

'I promise not to get in your way.'

But he was already in her way, Kate thought uncharitably. He was already a disturbing influence she could well have done without.

She stared at him in silent exasperation. When it came down to it, what grounds did she have to refuse? Like it or not, Sam was, after all, her boss and the sooner she got used to the idea the better.

'All right.' She glanced at her watch. 'But I warn you, I'm very busy and I'm leaving in five minutes, with or without—' She was wasting her breath. She looked up just in time to see him wave before the door closed behind him. Kate sighed heavily.

When she went out to the car park five minutes later he

was standing by the car, gazing up at a steadily brightening sky.

'So where are we off to first, then?'

'The Bensons. It's their youngest girl, Laura. I gather she's a bit chesty.'

'Fair enough. I thought it might be easier if we take my car. It will give me a chance to find my way around. You don't mind, do you?'

Kate jumped as his hand came beneath her elbow. In a small, nervous gesture she ran a hand through her hair. 'No, I suppose not.'

It wasn't a small car, but she was still aware of him, too close, could smell the distinctive musky aftershave he was wearing as she climbed reluctantly into the passenger seat. She averted her eyes, concentrating on the coastline, the silver path of sunlight across the sea.

'I'm sorry you're not happy about me joining the practice.'

She jumped as his voice broke into the silence. 'I didn't say that.'

'You didn't have to. You have a remarkably expressive face, Dr Dawson. The question that intrigues me is why?'

'Why?' She cleared her throat.

'Oh, I know how you feel about Doug leaving. But I sense there's more to it.' He turned his head to glance briefly in her direction. 'Is it something I've inadvertently done—or said?'

'I really don't know what you mean. Why should you think that?'

'I've no idea. Suppose you tell me.'

Her chin lifted. 'It isn't personal.'

'I'd like to believe that.' Sam's hands tightened briefly on the steering-wheel. 'I'm not looking for a fight, Kate. I'd just like to feel I was welcome here.'

'Maybe that's it.' She looked at him sharply. 'Why exactly are you here? I mean the real reason. Why Hellensey?'

His dark brows drew together. 'I would have thought that was fairly obvious.'

'Not to me. This is a tiny island. In the winter we're often cut off from the mainland.' She directed him into a narrow lane. 'The Bensons' place is ahead a couple of hundred yards. Why would you want to leave what you've been used to for—for this?' She gestured briefly at the green, shrub-covered cliffs and the small bay below. 'This is a different world.'

A spasm flickered briefly across his face. 'I suppose it was a series of coincidences. My contract with the VSO was coming up for renewal when I got some bad news from home. My mother was seriously ill. She'd been diagnosed with breast cancer.'

'Oh, no.' Kate felt her throat tighten. 'How awful. It must have been more difficult for you—being so far away.'

A muscle flickered in his jaw. 'I don't know that it was. In a way the decision was made for me. I came home. My father isn't particularly strong. I figured they needed all the moral support they could get.'

'I'm sure you were right,' Kate said quietly. 'I've seen patients go through it, of course. I don't know how anyone comes to terms with a thing like that.'

'I'm not sure that they do. They all deal with it in different ways.' He took his gaze briefly from the road to look at her. 'In my mother's case things were slightly more complicated. Apparently my maternal grandmother had died of breast cancer so my mother was faced with the option of having the one breast removed or going for a double mastectomy.'

'What a terrible choice to have to make,' Kate said softly.

Sam turned to look at her and smiled. 'Actually, she said it was probably the easiest decision she had ever had to make. She opted for the double mastectomy. Right now she's recovering nicely and knows she isn't going to have to face the fear in the future that the disease might come back again.'

'I'm not sure I'd have had her courage.'

'Given the same set of circumstances, I dare say you'd have made the same choice.' He smiled. 'So—in answer to your question—that's why I came back to England when I did. I took a couple of locum jobs, then I heard about Hellensey. It sounded ideal—something different and still close enough to home so that I can get there reasonably quickly should I need to. The contract suits me. Twelve months gives me time to consider my options.'

Kate bit at her lip. 'I'm sorry. I shouldn't have asked. I didn't mean to pry.'

'You had every right.' He turned his head slowly to look at her. 'It's not a problem, Kate. Since we're going to be working together we might as well get the niceties out of the way, don't you think?'

It was almost a relief when they drew up at the house a couple of minutes later.

June Benson led them into the sitting room. Forty years old, blonde-haired and slim, she looked harassed. With a slight laugh of embarrassment she stubbed out a cigarette in an ashtray. 'I know I shouldn't. I just can't seem to give them up.'

A window was open, letting in a cold draught of air. In the garden, ten-year-old Kevin was playing on a swing. Sitting curled up in a chair, watching television, his eight-year-old sister was wheezing badly. She looked flushed and was coughing.

'Here's Dr Dawson come to see you, Laura.' June Benson smiled wryly as she reached over to switch off the television. 'It's a nice day now that the rain's cleared. It seems a shame for her to be cooped up indoors but she's feeling quite poorly today, aren't you, poppet?'

Laura coughed again.

'Hello.' Kate smiled and sat on the couch beside the girl. 'We've met before, haven't we?' She turned to look at Sam. 'This is Dr Slater. He's come to join us at the practice.'

Sam smiled and held out his hand. 'I hope you don't mind, Laura. I'm new around here and I thought it might be a good opportunity to get to know some of our patients.'

'Two for the price of one. Now, that's what I really call service.' June Benson's hands shook as she lit another cigarette, closed her eyes and inhaled deeply.

Suppressing a sigh, Kate snapped open the locks of her briefcase and took out a stethoscope. 'Yes, well, now, Laura,' she said with a smile. 'So how long have you been feeling wheezy, then?'

'A few days.' The child smiled shyly. She was small for her age, pale, dark-haired and, Kate guessed, probably underweight.

'So you were feeling poorly at school?'

Laura glanced at her mother and nodded. 'Teacher said my cough sounded nasty. She asked if I'd been to the doctor.'

Her mother gave a sharp little laugh. 'Some of these teachers think you have nothing better to do than keep trotting back and forth.' The ash from her cigarette fell onto the carpet. 'Some of us have to work for a living,' she said defensively. 'I can't keep taking time off, can I? Not if I want to keep my job.'

'Where do you work, Mrs Benson?' Sam smiled.

'In a café, down by the harbour.' She exhaled another cloud of smoke. 'Of course, now that the summer trade has all but finished things are pretty quiet. I'll probably have to start looking for something else.'

'It can't be easy for you.'

The woman gave a short laugh. 'You can say that again. Oh, they've been pretty good to me, and I enjoy the work, but they don't like it when I keep having to take time off every time young Laura here has another one of her turns.'

'Yes, I can see it might cause problems. Let's just listen to your chest, shall we, Laura?' Kate applied her stethoscope to the child's chest, her gaze meeting Sam's as she listened to the familiar wheezing sounds. 'Right, and now let's take a look at your throat and ears. OK, well, that's not too bad.'

Kate patted the child's hand. 'I think you can go back to watching television now. Dr Slater and I will have a chat to Mummy.' She looked at the woman. 'Perhaps in the kitchen?'

'So, how is she, then?' June drew in a lungful of smoke.

'Well, actually, she's not too bad. She has a virus infection, which is why she has a temperature and is wheezing.'

The woman looked visibly relieved. 'So it's not another asthma attack, then?'

Kate shook her head. 'No, not this time. I can give you a prescription for some medicine for Laura to stop the wheezing.'

'Well, thank heaven for that. And what about school?'

'I'd give it a miss for a few days.' Kate smiled. 'By then she'll be over the worst of it. In the meantime, you can always give me a call at the surgery if she doesn't seem to be getting any better.'

She snapped the locks on her briefcase, handed the woman a prescription and rose to her feet. At the door she paused. 'And how about you, Mrs Benson? How are you feeling?'

The other woman gave a slight laugh. 'I manage. Don't have any choice, do I? It's like the maintenance. It sounds good but it never happens, and I'm left trying to explain to the kids why they can't have all the things their friends have.'

Kate nodded sympathetically. 'Yes, well if ever you feel you need to talk, you know where to reach me.'

Five minutes later they were back in the car. With a wry grin Sam opened the car windows slightly. 'Just to get rid of the smell of cigarette smoke. It clings rather.'

'I have spoken to her about her smoking.' Kate sighed, glad of the cooling breeze. 'She knows it isn't helping Laura's asthma.'

'But Mum needs to smoke.' Sam turned his head to glance in her direction. 'An interesting case, I thought.'

'You did?'

'Didn't you?'

'Maybe I'm too close to it.' Kate pushed a strand of hair behind her ear. 'Doug had to admit young Laura to hospital last winter when she had a particularly bad asthma attack. From the case notes it looks as if he probably saw her twice, maybe three times this summer and I saw her once when I happened to be on call.'

'Obviously you're worried about her.'

'Wouldn't you be?'

'That rather depends.' He frowned. 'What happened to the father? I take it there is a Mr Benson?'

'If there is he's pretty elusive. I've certainly never met

him. From the little that's been said, I got the impression that Mrs Benson is the only breadwinner and she's not too happy about it.'

'I can't say I blame her.'

'No, neither do I.'

'So you don't know when he left the scene?'

'I think Doug once vaguely mentioned the family. It must have been two...two and a half years ago. Yes, I'm pretty sure he was called out to an incident. Some kind of domestic violence. Mrs Benson ended up in Casualty and Joe Benson did a runner and they've been chasing him for maintenance payments ever since.'

Sam's mouth curved in a wry smile. 'Marital bliss.'

'Tell me about it.' She was conscious of Sam glancing briefly in her direction. The light was fading now, changing the colour of the sea from dark blue to pewter grey.

He was silent for a moment, concentrating on the narrow road, before he said, 'How long has Laura been having these asthma attacks?'

'I suppose...a couple of years. Why?' Kate glanced at him. 'You don't think there's a connection between the domestic disputes and young Laura's asthma attacks?'

'Do you?'

She frowned. 'I suppose you could be right. Emotional upset can trigger an attack. I need to go over Doug's notes more thoroughly to see if some sort of pattern emerges.'

Her throat tightened as she turned her head to gaze out of the window. 'Why is it always the kiddies who get hurt? It's so damned unfair.'

He turned his head to look at her. 'Hey, come on. You can't let it get to you.'

Easy to say. But that was the problem. It *did* get to her. Even now, despite the years of medical training, she could still empathise with that small, frightened child.

She shrugged slightly. 'No, I expect you're right. But it's not always so easy, is it?'

'No. I don't suppose it is.' He manoeuvred the car out of a narrow lane, before turning to look at her. 'Are you all right?'

'What...?' She blinked. 'Oh, yes, fine. Tired, that's all.'

'It's been a long day.'

And then some, she thought.

It was another hour and dark before they finally headed back towards the practice. The late afternoon air already struck with a deepening chill. The surgery was in darkness. She'd forgotten it was half-day closing. She'd forgotten what *day* it was. Too much was changing too quickly.

Sam drew the car to a halt and turned off the engine, but made no attempt to get out. 'Here we are again. Home, sweet home.'

'What?' Kate blinked again. 'Oh, yes.' She gazed out of the window and frowned. 'Look, I'm sorry, I should have asked how you've settled in. Doug and Elizabeth used the cottage for a couple of years after they first arrived on the island, but they soon decided it was too small and rented a bigger place.'

'It suits me fine. I'm light on personal possessions and I'm not the world's best cook so I don't spend too much time in the kitchen.' He grinned. 'The tin opener and I are on the best of terms.'

A damning reflection on his wife, Kate thought. Assuming, of course, that there was a wife.

'How about you?' He turned slowly and she could feel the blue eyes studying her.

'I beg your pardon?'

'I take it you must live within easy driving distance of the practice?'

'Yes, I have a small cottage. Just down the road more or less.'

'And what about Mr Dawson?' He smiled. 'I take it there *is* a Mr Dawson?'

Kate turned away, making a play of gathering up her briefcase. 'As it happens, no, there isn't. Not any more.'

'I'm sorry.' He frowned. 'It seems it's my turn to pry. I shouldn't have asked.'

Her fingers tightened spasmodically. 'It's all right. It's no secret. You have every right to know. Colin and I were divorced just over two years ago.'

Some emotion flared briefly in the depths of his eyes. 'I really am sorry.'

'It happens.'

'Yes, but I don't suppose that makes it any easier, does it?'

'No.' She gave a short laugh. 'I suppose I should have seen it coming. History repeating itself, you might say.'

Sam's mouth tightened. 'In what way? Or would you rather not talk about it?'

'There's not much to tell.' She forced herself to look at him directly. 'My parents divorced after what, I later realised, must have been years of arguments and bitter rows. I suppose, at the time, I thought that was what happened in all families.' Her mouth twisted. 'I knew I didn't like what was happening but I thought it was all perfectly normal. Crazy, isn't it?'

'How old were you when it happened?'

Kate shrugged. 'Ten. Twelve when he walked out.'

'Old enough to know what was going on—too young to understand why.' He turned his head to look at her. 'Were you close to your father?'

'Yes. I missed him a lot. I suppose I blamed Mum. I can't have made life easy for her—' She broke off.

'You don't have to go on. I shouldn't have asked.'

Sighing, she lifted her head to look at him. 'It's all right. I don't mind talking about it.'

'But the business with the young Benson girl touched a nerve?'

'Yes, I suppose it did. I can understand what she must be going through—her mum, too.' She gave a slight laugh. 'I just didn't expect my own marriage to fall apart. I mean, don't they say lightning never strikes twice, and all that? Well, it certainly did in my case.' She grimaced. 'Perhaps I'm jinxed.'

'How did you meet?'

'At the hospital where I was training.' She drew a deep breath. 'Colin was a pharmacist and from the moment he saw me he came after me. I resisted at first. I thought he was a little too confident, too sure of himself.' She shrugged. 'The truth is, I suppose I was flattered. Oh, I knew he had a bit of a reputation and I told myself he wasn't my type. I wasn't going to fall for it, but the more I resisted the more he pursued me, and I was intrigued by him, fascinated by him... We married six months later and, as far as I was concerned, it was a marriage made in heaven.'

'What happened?'

She sighed. 'Colin found someone else. *Several* someone elses, in fact. It seems they were all fascinated by him.' She eased the tension in her neck muscles. 'I heard later that he'd actually been seeing someone within three months of our marriage, and the galling thing is that I was the last to know what was going on. Not much of a judge of character, am I?'

'You were hardly to blame.'

'No, but that didn't make it any easier.'

'And is that why you came to Hellensey?'

'It seemed like a good idea. I needed to make a fresh start, meet new people. Doug helped me through a bad time.'

'I can see why he was so special to you,' Sam said softly.

'Yes, well, as I said, it's all water under the bridge. It took me a while to realise that Colin was a bad mistake, but at least it's one I won't make again.' She glanced at her watch. 'It's getting late. I'd better go.' She turned and fumbled with the doorhandle.

'Kate, wait!'

She turned to find his face suddenly very close to her own. For several seconds she was held within the warm circle of his arm. His skin smelled faintly of aftershave and she was totally unprepared for the primitive way in which, for those few seconds, she seemed to respond to that brief contact.

She drew in a deep breath as his hand closed over hers, drawing her slowly, imperceptibly, closer. She became aware of his frowning gaze, of the sensual mouth just a breath away, so close that her nostrils were invaded by the clean, musky smell of him.

She closed her eyes as his thumb brushed briefly against her cheek, sending a riot of sensations running through her as his lips brushed gently against hers. He smelled of aftershave and danger, though she couldn't for the life of her have explained why.

She drew a deep breath, shivering slightly, and somehow, without her even being aware of it, he had released her.

Sam straightened up, frowning, and looked at his watch. 'You're right, it's getting late. Why don't you head for home? I still have some work to do here, so if anything else has cropped up that needs attention I'll deal with it.'

Seconds later she watched him drive away before heading towards her own car. It was galling to discover that her hands were actually shaking as she found the key and inserted it into the ignition. This was ridiculous! She didn't even know this man, so what was it about Sam Slater that was making her so irrationally edgy?

Breathing hard, Kate snapped the seat belt firmly into place and turned to stare out of the window, telling herself decisively that she wouldn't think about it—which wasn't easy when her pulse was still racing crazily out of control.

Kate drew in a sharp breath. For the first time in a long while a sudden feeling of loneliness swept through her, threatening to overwhelm her in its intensity. Damn him! Damn Sam Slater!

She had spent the two years since Colin's betrayal trying to pick up the pieces, and was just beginning to get her life into some sort of order. She didn't know anything about Sam, except that he had walked, uninvited, into her life and that he seemed to provoke a great many conflicting emotions in her, none of which was going to make for an easy working relationship.

CHAPTER THREE

KATE brushed droplets from her hair as she put her briefcase on the floor in Reception. 'Ugh! It's pouring with rain out there.'

Lucy greeted Kate's arrival with a smile. 'Wouldn't you just know it? The visitors certainly know when to leave the island, don't they?'

'I'm beginning to wish I could join them.' Kate nodded in the direction of the waiting room. 'Is it busy out there or dare I hope they've all decided to be sensible and stay home?'

'No chance!' Lucy grinned. 'Actually, it's not too bad. We've had a couple of cancellations. Probably the weather is putting a few people off.' She flipped through the appointments diary. 'Oh, yes, Mrs Thomas rang to say that the swelling on young Matthew's ankle seems to be going down and she didn't want to bring him in unnecessarily. I said if she was at all worried to give us a call.'

'That's fine.' Kate reached for the bundle of letters on the desk.

'And Mr...Jameson.' Lucy tapped the page. 'He had an appointment at ten-thirty but can't make it after all. Something about a visit to his solicitor. I've shifted him to tomorrow, I hope that's all right?'

'It sounds fine. If only all our problems were so easily solved. Is that it?'

Lucy gave a rueful smile. 'The bad news is we had a call from Mrs Walker.'

Kate frowned. 'I take it it's about her husband?'

'Yes. Apparently his breathing wasn't too good yesterday and he had a bad night. She's quite worried about him. Do you want me to sort out his notes for you?'

Kate nodded. 'Please, if you would. I'll call in to see him later.' She leaned over the desk. 'Is that my list for this morning?'

'Afraid so.' She handed over the piece of paper. 'It looks like being a busy one.'

'When isn't it?' Kate smiled wryly. 'Well, I suppose I'd better make a start, then.' Gathering up her briefcase and the bundle of case notes, she felt her gaze drawn involuntarily to the small office where Sam stood at the window, engaged in an animated conversation with Jill.

Dressed in dark trousers and a short-sleeved shirt, there was an aura of powerful masculinity about Sam that took her breath away. She watched as he threw back his head, giving a deep-throated laugh. Absorbed in her own critical survey, she suddenly became aware that his own eyes were appraising her in turn.

It was a disconcerting feeling. Illogically it made her want to check that her mascara hadn't run, or that a wisp of hair hadn't escaped from its restraining clip.

'Good morning.'

'Good morning.' She felt oddly flustered. 'I wasn't expecting to see you until later.'

'I've more or less sorted out the cottage. I figured the easiest and quickest way to familiarise myself with things around here was to *be* here.'

'Yes, well…' She turned away and said briskly to Lucy, 'Just give me a couple of minutes to sort myself out, will you? Then you can send in the first patient.'

'Will do. Uh-oh. Here we go again. Gables Surgery.' Lucy tucked the receiver under her chin as she hunted for a pen, shifting papers and files. 'Yes, Mrs Collins. It's young Sophie, is it? Yes, we are pretty busy but I'm sure the doctor will put you on her list of visits.' She looked questioningly at Kate, who nodded, before heading along the corridor to her consulting room.

On the way she met Tim.

'Hi. How're you doing?'

'Fine.' She grinned. 'Day off, is it?'

'I should be so lucky. There's enough paperwork on my desk to keep the European Union going for a couple of years. I reckon the stuff breeds.'

Kate laughed. 'Tell me about it.' She looked at her watch and groaned. 'I'd better make a start on my own contribution, see if I can't generate a little more. See you later.'

Minutes later she checked her appearance in the mirror—fashionable, straight, knee-length skirt, vivid, terracotta-coloured silk shirt.

Seating herself at the desk, she hitched her skirt into place and pressed the buzzer, summoning her first patient of the day.

The morning passed remarkably quickly. There was the inevitable spate of sore throats and coughs, which could be treated simply with aspirin and the old-fashioned but still useful remedy of hot honey and lemon, though a few required antibiotics.

Quickly draining a cup of nearly cold coffee, Kate pressed the buzzer again.

Maureen Lewis was about thirty years old. She and her family—husband Ted and a lively five-year old—had moved to the island about eighteen months ago to open a small craft shop, producing local pottery.

The woman was coughing. She looked flushed and not too happy.

'Hello, Mrs Lewis.' Smiling, Kate gestured her towards the chair. 'How's the business going?'

'Oh, pretty well. We had a good season. The warm weather brought the tourists over to the island so we should at least break even.'

'Well, that's good news.'

Maureen smiled. 'The bank will certainly be pleased, and it's a weight off our minds. We thought it might take a couple of seasons to get going properly, so it's better than we dared hope for. Ted's relieved. I know he was worried.'

'And what about you? How are you feeling?'

'I've got this awful sore throat, and a cough. It's a real nuisance.'

Kate brought up the patient's notes on her computer screen. This was only the second time Maureen had been in to see her since she'd moved to the island. Her first visit had been to ask for an ongoing supply of her contraceptive pills. Other than that, her health generally seemed good.

'How long have you been coughing?'

'Oh, I suppose...about a week. I thought it would go but it seems to be getting worse.'

'Well, let's take a look at your throat and see if we can find out what's going on. Does that hurt there?'

She made a gentle but thorough examination and Maureen winced. 'Ouch!'

Kate nodded sympathetically. 'Your glands are swollen and your throat is slightly red.' Tossing the throat spatula into the bin, Kate rinsed her hands at the sink, before returning to her desk. 'I think what you've got is an upper respiratory tract infection, probably viral.'

'At least that explains why I've been feeling so awful.'

'Yes, it's not very nice.'

'Still, I dare say antibiotics will soon put it right. They sort out most things, don't they?'

Kate frowned slightly. It was a depressing fact that a lot of patients firmly believed that antibiotics were the panacea for all ills and the only means to recovery. Part of her job seemed to be to convince them that it wasn't always the case.

'The problem is that antibiotics are really quite useless where viruses are concerned,' she explained, smiling sympathetically.

'You mean you can't give me anything?'

Kate stifled a sigh. 'Most viruses run a natural course. I know it can be pretty uncomfortable for a while but, I promise you, they do clear up eventually without medication.'

Maureen was clearly not impressed. 'So you're saying I can't have antibiotics?'

'The trouble is that antibiotics can sometimes produce problems in themselves,' Kate said patiently.

'Like what?'

'Well, like thrush, for instance, or diarrhoea. At worst, in extremely rare cases, some people have an allergic, possibly life-threatening reaction to certain antibiotics. So you see, there are very good reasons why doctors are sometimes reluctant to prescribe particular drugs.'

She smiled. 'One other reason most doctors are reluctant to prescribe antibiotics is because, in the event that you might need them for a more serious condition, they might not work because your body will have become immune to the drugs. So, although it seems unfair, I really am trying to do what is best.'

Maureen Lewis frowned. 'I appreciate what you're saying, but the fact is I still have a business to run. I can't afford to take time off. All I need is something to make me feel better.'

'I can appreciate that.' Kate sat back in her chair and looked at the woman. 'Look, what I suggest is that you go home and rest. Yes, I know…' Kate smiled. 'It isn't easy, but I want you to take paracetamol or aspirin, whichever suits you best. That should help to bring your temperature down and relieve the aches and pains. Drink as much fluid as you can and try steam inhalations to relieve the cough. If you're not feeling better in three days, or if you're at all worried, come back and see me.'

She watched as the woman left then summoned her next patient. Mary Duncan was forty-five years old. Kate had come to know her quite well in the past couple of years. If there were any social events to be organised on the island, Mary Duncan, despite having three growing children, could always be guaranteed to be at the centre of things—always busy, always cheerful. So it came as something of a shock to Kate to see her now.

The woman looked pale and tired as she moved stiffly to sit in the chair.

Kate frowned. 'You're not looking well, Mary. What can I do for you?'

The woman ran a hand wearily through her hair and made a feeble attempt at a smile. 'I wouldn't mind a few energy pills if you've got some. I don't know what the matter is with me. I just feel so tired all the time and it's not like me. I seem to find it so hard to concentrate.'

'When did you first notice the symptoms?'

'Oh—back in the summer.' Mary gave a slight laugh. 'I didn't take too much notice at first. You know how it is. Loads to do. Kids on holiday. I thought it might be my age—hitting forty-five and it's all downhill from here.'

Kate laughed. 'I don't think your age has anything to do with it. You've always been full of energy and reasonably healthy.' She glanced at her computer notes. 'In fact, judging from these, I'd say you were healthier than most. You hardly ever come to the surgery.'

'I know. I think that's why it's harder to accept that I don't seem to be able to do all the things I want to do.'

'Yes, I can see that it must be frustrating for you.'

'What I can't cope with is feeling so weepy all the time. I mean, it's really not like me.'

'Apart from the mood changes, how do you feel otherwise? Any aches and pains?'

Mary Duncan gave a short laugh. 'My joints ache. I keep getting headaches—awful headaches—and hot flushes. Tom says I'm ready for the knacker's yard.' Her expression changed. 'I'm beginning to think he's right.'

Kate shook her head. 'Whatever it is, we're going to sort it out. You'll be fine.'

'I wish I could believe it. I'm sure I could cope if only I didn't feel so tired. Can't you just give me some pills—a tonic, or some vitamins, or something?'

Kate's mouth curved in a wry response. 'I probably could, but what we really need to do is get to the bottom of what's causing the symptoms.' She frowned. 'Have you had a rash of any kind?'

'Well, now that you mention it, yes. These red rings came up on my arms.' She eased back the sleeve of her sweater, revealing her upper arms. 'I first noticed them up here. They weren't too bad to begin with, but they gradually got worse.'

Kate rose to her feet to make a gentle examination. 'Mmm, they don't look very nice, do they?'

'Oh, they're not so bad now.' Mary glanced at Kate. 'You don't think this could have anything to do with the other symptoms, do you?'

'It's possible.' Returning to her desk, Kate glanced again at her notes. 'You haven't had a blood test recently, have you?'

'No. Why? Do you think I should? You don't think...? I mean, it's not anything serious, is it?'

Kate smiled. 'No, I'm sure it isn't, except that it's obviously serious in that it's affecting your life.'

'So, can you give me some cream or something for the rash? Some antibiotics, maybe?'

Kate frowned. 'I'd really rather not prescribe antibiotics, Mary, until we know precisely what we're dealing with. Look, I'm going to send you for a blood test.'

'Does that mean you don't know what's wrong with me?'

'I have an idea, but I really want to be sure.' Kate smiled and scribbled a note. 'If you pop along to see the nurse now, she'll be able to take the blood and, hopefully, we'll get the results in a few days' time. So if you arrange another appointment when you go through Reception, I'll see you again, and by then I'm pretty sure we'll know exactly how to tackle the problem once and for all.'

Half an hour later, having seen the last of her patients, Kate headed for the office. Something about Mary Duncan's symptoms was nagging at the back of her mind. If only she could put her finger on just what was causing them.

Frowning, she scanned the rows of books on the bookshelves. She had flicked through several when she was vaguely aware of the door opening and Sam entering the room. He put his briefcase down and glanced at his list of calls, before frowning in her direction.

'Problems?'

'I'm not sure.' Her breathing was suddenly uneven, but, then, it always seemed to be whenever he was around. She drew herself up sharply. 'It's annoying really. It's a woman I saw this morning. Her symptoms have been bothering her for weeks. She's obviously not well. I just can't put my finger on what's causing the problem.'

'What sort of symptoms?'

Kate snapped the book to a close and raked a hand through her hair. 'That's part of the problem, they're pretty varied.'

He smiled slightly. 'Such as?'

'Oh, headaches, muscle stiffness, aching joints, hot flushes.'

'And how old is the patient?'

'Mid-forties.'

'And you've considered…'

'That she might be menopausal?' Kate frowned. 'Yes, of course I have and I'm convinced it isn't that.'

Sam half sat on the desk. He had taken off his jacket, and was carrying it slung over one shoulder, revealing tautly muscled arms and chest beneath his open-necked shirt. 'Have you done a blood test?'

'Yes.' Kate swallowed hard and averted her gaze. 'I just have this feeling that I'm missing something, something obvious.'

'Well, the symptoms you've mentioned so far could be due to any number of things.' He frowned. 'Is there a rash?'

She nodded. 'Yes, and it's been getting worse. And yes…' she gave a wry smile '…I've eliminated most of the usual, childhood-type things such as measles or chickenpox.'

'Hmm. I can see that it's a bit baffling.'

'A bit!' Kate returned the books to the shelf. 'I've never come across anything quite like it before.'

'What other symptoms has she mentioned?'

'Oh—diarrhoea, loss of appetite, feeling weepy.'

Sam frowned. 'I suppose you've considered Lyme disease?'

'Lyme disease?' She stared at him then gave a short laugh. 'No, I hadn't, but now that you mention it...'

Sam crossed to the bookshelf. Frowning, he glanced through the titles and selected a volume. 'Sue was right. We do need some more up-to-date reference books. Here.' He flipped through the pages and handed the book to her. 'I could be wrong, but I'd say Lyme disease is what you're looking for or, at the very least, it's worth considering.'

Kate read the text, gave a sigh of exasperation and looked at him. 'I can't believe I didn't see it.'

His slow smile did things to her already overworked pulse rate. 'It's not exactly common. The chances of anyone catching Lyme disease is probably one in ten thousand.'

She laughed. 'I'll tell Mary Duncan that. I'm sure she'll appreciate it.'

'In fact, it was first diagnosed in Lyme, Connecticut, about twenty-five years ago. That's where it got its name. It's caused by a tick bite. Infection usually occurs between spring and early autumn.'

'Well, thank heavens one of us knows something about it.' She smiled hesitantly. 'Look, I'm grateful. It could have taken me weeks to come up with an answer.'

'I doubt it. The blood test would have put you on the right track.'

'Yes. Well, at least now I can get her started on a course of antibiotics.'

'It's going to be a long job. Could be six weeks or more.'

'I don't think Mary will mind that, knowing that she's finally going to start feeling well again.'

Sam grinned. 'I think we've earned a cup of coffee, don't you? Maybe even a biscuit to go with it.'

Kate glanced at her watch. 'I'm not sure...'

'Five minutes. Let's call it lunch.' In one fluid movement

he moved to hold the door open. 'Here, you may need these.' He swept up her keys and placed them in her hands.

Kate felt the breath catch in her throat as a feeling of physical awareness swept through her, then she pulled her hands out of his grasp. 'Thanks.'

'Think nothing of it.' His gaze narrowed briefly. 'Coffee?'

The staffroom was full as they entered. Tim was dispensing coffee, Jill inspecting the latest medical journal and Sue sank into a chair, kicking off her shoes before stifling a jaw-cracking yawn. 'Lord, I need a holiday.'

'Don't we all?' Lucy eyed a plate of biscuits, patted her waistline, sighed and resisted the temptation. 'Better not if I'm going to get into my new winter clothes in a few weeks' time.'

'Talking of clothes—and other things—' Jill glanced at Tim as she spooned sugar into her coffee. 'How's Theresa bearing up under the strain?'

He grinned. 'Remarkably well, apart from a sudden attack of nerves about taking a couple of weeks off when she knows the maternity unit is going to be rushed off their feet.'

'When aren't they?' Kate smiled. 'Mind you, they do say September and October are the worst months.'

'It's all the Christmas babies.' Sue helped herself to a chocolate biscuit, broke it and handed half to Lucy. 'Here. This way we both ease our consciences. So...' She looked at Tim. 'Only a couple of weeks to go now to the big day. And you're looking disgustingly calm, Dr Blake. Shouldn't you be feeling just a shade nervous?'

'Not me, mate.' Tim grinned. 'Can't come soon enough for me.'

Helping himself to strong, black coffee, Sam stood with

his back to the window. 'Do I take it someone's getting married soon?'

'Not so that you'd notice.' Sue laughed. 'The fair Theresa decided to make an honest man of our Dr Blake. Can't for the life of me imagine why.'

'Just ask every female patient on his list.' Jill gave an exaggerated sigh. 'They all think he's the dishiest thing ever. Can't see it myself.'

'Hey, come on, girls. Give a bloke a break, can't you?'

'I suppose you do realise your popularity quotient is going to drop like a stone once there's a *Mrs* Blake?'

'Yeah, well.' He laughed. 'You can't please all the folk all of the time.' Tim looked at Sam. 'Seriously, though, I reckon this is going to drop you in it a bit, what with me taking time off just when things are hotting up here. Trouble is, when we made our plans none of us had figured on Doug leaving the practice.'

Sam had moved to half sit, half lean against the table. 'It's not a problem. I'm sure Kate and I will cope, won't we?' His glance locked with hers. 'I think we'll manage to get along, don't you, Dr Dawson?'

He smiled and with a start Kate realised he was laughing at her. A small pulse began to throb in her throat.

'Oh, I think we can just about manage not to come to blows.' She leapt to her feet to rescue her cup from Tim. 'I'll do that, shall I? Anyone else for a refill?'

'I wouldn't mind.'

She willed her hands to remain steady as she poured more coffee. Having done so, she turned, handing Sam the cup, and as he took it their fingers met. The memory of the few seconds she had spent in his arms came surging back so vividly that she jerked away, spilling coffee into the saucer.

'Come to think of it...' Tim unwittingly came to her

rescue. 'I'm having a bit of a blokes' night out. Just a few friends. Why don't you join us? You'd be more than welcome.'

'Well…' Sam frowned. 'That's very kind of you, but, well, I…'

'It's not going to be a big bash. Just a few beers.'

'Are you getting married locally?'

'No.' Tim grinned. 'We thought we'd do things in style and fly out to the sun to get married. Well, it made sense really. My folks can't be at the wedding, worse luck, not since Dad had his stroke a couple of years back. So we thought we might as well get away from the British weather for a while.'

'We should all be so lucky.' Sue grinned.

'Anyway, you're welcome to come and join us for a tinny or two.'

'Well, if you're sure…?'

'Absolutely, mate. As I said, it's a blokes' night really but if there's someone you'd like to bring along, feel free.'

Without turning her head, Kate could feel the weight of Sam's blue eyes watching her, his own expression giving nothing away as she turned slowly.

Without being aware of it, her fingers tightened round the cup. 'Perhaps you'd better discuss it with someone. Your… Mrs Slater, perhaps?' The words were out before she had even had time to think about it.

She saw the muscle tighten in his jaw. Jill's cup clattered noisily into the saucer. Kate shot a quick glance in Tim's direction and saw a derisive smile tugging at the corners of his mouth.

Sam smiled wryly. 'It's a nice idea. Unfortunately my mother is with my father on a boat, sailing up the Nile, at this precise moment. I doubt if she would be too impressed if I phoned her right now.'

Lucy sniggered and Kate felt the warm colour rise in her cheeks.

'Look, I'm sorry. I didn't mean to—'

'It's not a problem,' Sam said coolly. He looked at Tim. 'As a matter of fact, I'd love to come, provided I'm not on duty at the time, of course. And now…' he glanced at his watch '…I must make a move or I'm not going to get back in time for this evening's surgery.'

He was gone and Kate turned to Tim, with an effort keeping her voice even.

'Why do I get the feeling I said the wrong thing?'

Tim frowned. 'Obviously you don't know.'

'Obviously I don't.' She stared at him, her mouth suddenly dry. 'What *should* I know?'

'That Sam was engaged. She died about a month before they were due to be married.'

CHAPTER FOUR

STANDING outside Sam's room, Kate raised her hand, hesitated for a second, then knocked. It was disconcerting to find her hand shaking as she fumbled with the doorhandle.

Sam was sitting at his desk. Kate swallowed hard.

'Sam, I'm so sorry. I had no right to say what I did...'

'Forget it. It isn't important.' He pushed a pile of papers aside and rose to his feet.

'I can't forget it,' she said flatly, feeling the colour darken her cheeks as she looked at him. 'Tim told me about your fiancée. I had no idea.'

'There's no reason why you should,' he said evenly. 'It's all right, Kate. Hannah died over two years ago. I've come to terms with it.'

'It can't have been easy.'

'No.' His mouth twisted.

'Can you talk about it?'

'Yes. It took a while, but it's true what they say—time does lessen the pain.' He gave a wry smile. 'Not that you believe that at the time, of course.'

'No, I can understand that.' She swallowed hard. 'How old was she?'

He frowned. 'She was twenty-five when it happened. That's what made it seem worse.'

'Was she a doctor?'

He shook his head. 'No. She was a children's nurse. She loved her work and she should have had her whole life ahead of her and then, because of some damned accident...' He ran a hand through his hair. 'I wasn't there at the time, but it seems that a child fell in the river. Hannah went in after him.' He gave a slight laugh. 'That was typical of her. She always was impulsive.'

Kate moistened her dry lips with her tongue. 'Sam, you don't have to do this. I shouldn't have asked...'

'It really is all right. There's no reason why you shouldn't know.' He gave a tight smile. 'Yes, I still get angry when I think about it—the awful waste. But at least I *can* talk about it now.' He turned away and stood gazing out of the window.

'She managed to save the child, but the river was high and fast-running after a storm. The boy was pulled onto the bank but Hannah was swept away before anyone could get to her. It was another twenty-four hours before they found her body.'

Kate drew a ragged breath. 'I...I don't know what to say.'

'This isn't your fault, Kate. Like I said, at the time I didn't think I'd ever get over it.'

'That sounds like a perfectly natural reaction to me.'

'I'm sure it is. But you can't carry grief around with you for ever. Sooner or later you have to move on. *Life* has to go on. We don't have any choice and the pain does get less eventually. You must know that?' He moved to stack a pile of medical journals on a shelf.

Kate swallowed hard. She was conscious of his nearness. He was close enough for her to catch the faint scent of his cologne and feel the warmth emanating from his long, lean body as he glanced at her.

'Is...is that why you went abroad?'

'Let's say it made the decision easier. I was offered a job with the VSO. It seemed like a challenge and that was what I needed just then—a chance to get away and make a fresh start away from everything familiar, even the people

Hannah and I had known. Oh, they were all kind and well meaning, but the last thing I needed was sympathy. Does that sound crazy?'

'No, I don't think so. I suppose I felt pretty much the same after Colin left. People meant well but they didn't really understand how I felt—the sense of hurt and betrayal.'

With an effort Kate managed to force a smile to her lips. 'You must find all of this very different to what you saw in Africa.'

'Oh, I don't know. It's not really so very different. Sick people are the same anywhere. They get frightened. They need care and reassurance. But, yes, I suppose in a way it's different.'

He gave a slight smile. 'We take an awful lot for granted, Kate. Simple things like running water, electricity. It takes guts to give up the kind of things we take for granted every day of our lives to go and work in a place like Ramindi, and I'm not talking about myself. God knows, I only made a small contribution to what's happening out there. I'm talking about the kind of people who stay. Some of them give a lifetime's commitment.'

'Were you the only doctor at Ramindi?'

He laughed. 'No, thank God. When I arrived at the clinic there was a team of six—all nationalities. Nurses, a physio. Dr Dupres originally set up the clinic about four years ago, during which time they managed to recruit some of the locals as orderlies. Some of them are now training to be qualified nurses themselves.' He frowned. 'Needless to say, demand always outstripped resources.'

Kate smiled. 'It sounds like quite a project. This Dr...Dupres must be quite a character. I imagine he was pleased to have you join the team.'

A smile touched his mouth. 'I suppose she was.'

'She!' Kate flushed. 'Oh, I thought... I just...'

Sam grinned. 'Did what most people still do—make assumptions.'

'Yes, well...' She grinned sheepishly and glanced at the framed photograph on his desk. It showed an attractive, tanned, blonde-haired woman of about thirty, surrounded by a group of smiling African children. 'Is that her?'

Sam picked up the photograph and smiled as he smoothed his finger over its surface. 'Yes, that's Marie-Laure and some of her babies, as she calls them.'

For some reason Kate's mouth suddenly felt dry. With an effort she forced a smile. 'She sounds like quite a lady.'

'And then some!' He smiled. 'A five-foot-nothing whirlwind. That clinic wouldn't have happened without her.'

Kate said softly, 'I get the feeling she's rather special.'

'You could say.' Sam's dark brows drew together. 'Marie-Laure managed to make me see that life goes on, that it's still worth living. And she was right. If I had any doubts at all, I only had to look at those people, especially the children, to see that I was one of the lucky ones. She didn't offer sympathy. She gave me a job and, more important, she gave me a new purpose in life. I'll always be grateful for that.'

'You must miss her—and Ramindi.'

'Yes, of course I do. I miss them both. Working in a place like Ramindi, among those people, you can't help but build up strong relationships. But we keep in touch and, yes, Africa is the sort of place that grows on you. It may sound trite, but it really does have its own kind of magic.'

Kate felt her heart give an illogical extra thud. 'So... I suppose you'll be going back?'

He frowned. 'There's still a lot of work to do out there, and some wonderful people who need all the help they can get.'

'And Dr Dupres? Will she stay on in Ramindi?'

'I don't think she's made that decision yet. It's not an easy one to make. She may have other plans.'

Like marriage, for instance? Kate was shocked to feel an unreasoning twist of emotion which, she told herself, couldn't possibly be jealousy.

This is ridiculous, she thought as she straightened up briskly in self-disgust. What was she thinking of? She hardly knew this man. What Sam Slater chose to do with his life was of no interest to her whatsoever.

She looked at her watch. 'Oh, lor, is that the time?'

Jill tapped at the door and popped her head round. 'Oh, Kate, I thought I heard your voice. I'm glad I caught you. I've just had a call from Mrs Matthews. She's worried about her neighbour, Ed Bristow. You know, the old chap who lives at Hilltop Farm?'

Kate was instantly totally professional. 'What's the problem?'

'She's not sure, except that he seems a bit confused. It seems she called round yesterday and he was still wearing pyjamas. He didn't seem to know what time of day it was. She's obviously quite concerned.'

'I'll call and see him. I'm going out that way anyway. Can you sort out his cards for me?'

'Will do.'

'Perhaps I should tag along?'

Stifling a tiny and what she knew was a totally illogical feeling of resentment, Kate's head jerked up as Sam was already gathering up his briefcase.

'I really don't see the necessity,' she said briskly. 'I think I'm perfectly capable—'

'I'm not suggesting otherwise, Kate,' came the quiet rejoinder. 'It simply occurred to me that it might help if the next time Mrs Matthews feels concerned about her neighbour I know just a little about the situation, don't you think?'

'I suppose you're right.' She gave a slight sigh. 'Actually, I'll be glad of some moral support. Ed Bristow is nearly eighty and as tough as old boots, or at least he was until this past twelve months or so.'

'Is there a problem?'

She frowned. 'He had quite a nasty bout of bronchitis last winter. Since then I'm afraid, healthwise, he's been finding it all a bit of a battle. Ideally he'd be better off living with a relative or in warden-controlled accommodation where he can retain a measure of independence whilst knowing someone is on call. Either that...' she looked at Sam '...or we have to persuade him to accept more help. But he's already rejected that idea out of hand.'

'Is there a relative who would have him?'

'Ah—well, there's the rub. I've heard mention of a daughter, but she hasn't put in an appearance.'

Sam grinned. 'All in all, I have to say I don't much fancy your chances.'

'Nor do I.'

'Come on, I'll drive. You can tell me about Ed Bristow as we go.'

Minutes later she slid into the passenger seat beside him. As they headed along the narrow lanes, Kate studied him unhappily. 'I'm really not looking forward to this. The trouble is I know what the logical solution would be, as far as Ed is concerned, but he can be very stubborn.'

'Perhaps, between us, we can persuade him.'

Kate glanced at him. 'If Ed decides he wants to stay where he is, nothing will shift him, and I don't want him bullied.'

A spasm flickered briefly across Sam's face as he turned his head briefly to look at her. 'Whatever else you may think of me, Kate, I'm not a bully,' he said softly. 'I'm just as keen as you are for elderly people to retain their independence. In Ed Bristow's case, the priority is obviously that he can do so safely. I think we both have a professional responsibility in that respect, don't you?'

Kate bit her lip and was still pondering the problem when they reached the cottage a few minutes later.

Mrs Matthews must have been watching for them because she opened the door just as they reached it. 'Oh, Dr Dawson. I'm so glad you could come. I'm really quite worried about Ed.'

'It was good of you to take the trouble to call, Mrs Matthews. This is my colleague, Dr Slater, by the way.'

'Doctor.' Pat Matthews smiled as she led them to the small sitting room. A fire crackled in the hearth, the flames casting a small patch of brightness into the early gloom of the afternoon.

'How has he been?' Kate asked. 'I gather, from your message, that he seemed confused?'

'Well, he didn't seem too bad really until a couple of days ago,' Pat said quietly, picking up a plate from the small table. 'I made him a spot of lunch, just as I always do, and brought it over. Ed's always been partial to home-made soup, but he's hardly touched it today.' She rested a hand lightly on the shoulder of the man dozing in the chair. 'Ed, the doctor's here to see you.'

Kate looked at Ed Bristow and felt a tiny ripple of shock run through her. Despite his eighty years, he had continued to work in his garden and had always retained an air of fierce independence. Now, suddenly—overnight, it seemed—he had become a tiny, vulnerable old man.

She glanced briefly at Sam before putting her briefcase on the floor. Sitting in the chair opposite, she leaned forward, gently reaching out to hold one frail hand, her fingers registering the rapid pulse.

'Ed, it's Dr Dawson. Can you hear me?' She smiled as the paper-thin lids flickered open. 'I hear you haven't been feeling too well.'

Ed blinked and looked round the room. 'What's happening?' He wiped the back of his hand across his mouth and struggled to sit up.

'It's all right, Ed.' Pat handed him a glass of water, helping him as he sipped thirstily. She smiled. 'You remember Dr Dawson, don't you?'

Ed shook his head. 'Didn't send for the doctor.'

'No, *I* asked her to call, Ed. You haven't been feeling too well. I thought she could perhaps just take a look at you, make sure you're all right.'

'Can you tell me what's wrong, Ed?' Kate asked. 'Do you have any pain anywhere?'

Brown eyes clouded with confusion. 'No. Bit of a cough, that's all.' He tapped his fingers briefly against his chest. 'Don't need a doctor. I'm all right.'

'Don't worry about it, Ed,' Kate said gently. 'Do you know what day it is, Ed? Can you remember?'

The watery eyes gazed at her. 'Day? Aye, it's... I don't know. What do you want to know that for?'

Smiling, she patted his hand. 'It's not important. Don't worry about it. Now, as I'm here anyway, why don't I just listen to your chest? Is that all right? It won't take long.'

She took the stethoscope Sam held out to her, tilting a brief smile in his direction before making a gentle but thorough examination. A few seconds later she straightened up.

'Well, I'm afraid you've got a bit of an infection bubbling away in there again, Ed. That would explain why you're not feeling too well.'

His hand flapped her away. 'I'm all right. Can't stand fuss. Just leave me alone.'

'Mrs Matthews says you haven't been eating properly, Ed,' Sam said softly. 'She's worried about you.'

'I'm not hungry.'

'But you need to eat, Ed.' Kate frowned. 'If you don't eat you'll get weak. That's probably why you're feeling so poorly.' She looked at Sam and gave a slight sigh. 'I really think you need to go into hospital for a while, Ed, just to try to get this infection sorted out and build up your strength again.'

'I'm not going into any hospital.' His hands gripped the chair and she was shocked to see tears well up in his eyes. 'I'll be all right. I've got Pat to look after me. I want to stay here.'

'All right, Ed,' Kate said gently. She flung a glance at Sam and nodded briefly. He moved to hold one of the old man's thin hands.

'Hello, Ed. I'm Dr Slater. We've never met but I came to take over from Dr Parker. Do you remember him?'

'Aye.' Ed wiped his eyes. 'But I'm not going into hospital.'

'We don't want to force you to do anything you don't want to do, Ed. But you know that cough isn't going to get better without some help.'

'I can take tablets. Just give me what I had before.'

'Yes, I'm sure you can. The thing is, though, Ed, you need to take them regularly, four times a day, otherwise they won't make you better.' Sam smiled gently. 'Do you think you can manage to remember to take them, Ed. It's important.'

Ed turned his head away.

'I do know how you feel about going into hospital, Ed.'

'No, lad, you don't.' The old man wiped the back of his

hand across his eyes, before fumbling shakily in his pocket for a hanky. 'My Doris went into hospital. She didn't come out again. They said not to worry, but she died.'

'It's not the same, Ed,' Pat said gently. 'Your Doris had a problem with her heart. Don't you remember?' She glanced at Kate and said quietly, 'Doris was his wife. She had a heart attack late one night. They rushed her to the hospital but it was too late.'

Sam gently squeezed Ed's hand before straightening up. He shot a look in Kate's direction, nodding almost imperceptibly towards the door.

'He's working himself up into a state, Sam.'

He lowered his voice as they moved away fractionally. 'You're not happy about him, are you?'

'Are you?' Kate looked at him and he shook his head.

'No. Chest infections in a patient of his age can be more dangerous than in someone younger.'

'It would certainly account for the temperature.' Kate ran a hand through her hair. 'The fact that he isn't eating doesn't help. I can understand why he doesn't want to eat, but he's getting weaker.'

'What do you want to do?'

Her mouth twisted wryly. 'Ideally I'd like to get him into hospital, but I don't think it's going to happen, not without upsetting him. He's obviously dead set against it and I'm not going to force him.'

'I agree,' Sam said evenly. 'Which leaves the antibiotics.'

'*If* we can be sure he'll take them.'

'It's serious, isn't it?' Pat asked anxiously as she joined them. 'I've watched him getting steadily worse over the past couple of days, but he's such a stubborn old chap. He refused to let me call the surgery. Today he seemed worse.

It's just that I can't watch him all the time, not with the kids and all…'

'There's nothing you could do anyway,' Kate said gently.

'But we can't just leave him like this.'

'No, obviously not.'

'What about organising the back-up services?' Sam suggested. 'Someone who could pop in on a daily basis, do a bit of cleaning, see that he gets a proper meal?'

Pat gave a slight laugh. 'You'd be wasting your breath. I've suggested it several times. He just says they're a bunch of interfering busybodies and he won't have them. I've tried bringing him in a tray of food—a decent evening meal. He *says* he eats it but, as far as I can see, the only thing getting fatter around here is the cat.'

'Which leaves only one option.' Sam frowned. 'Try him on the antibiotics. Start him off with an initial injection. Give it two or three days and either we'll start to see an improvement or…'

Kate looked at Pat. 'Do you think you can persuade him to take tablets? It's important that he completes the course.'

'I can try. I pop in several times a day, anyway, to make him a nice hot drink. I can probably persuade him to swallow a couple of tablets at the same time.'

'So we'd better go for that, then.' Kate unlocked her briefcase, found a bottle of pills and handed it to the woman. 'I carry these with me, just in case. I'll give him an injection now but, if you can, persuade him to take a couple of these later tonight. By then, hopefully, he'll have calmed down a little.'

'Don't worry. Ed's no fool. I'm sure he realises he's only got two choices.'

'Does he have any relatives?'

Pat frowned. 'I did hear talk of a daughter, but I've been

here five years and we haven't seen any sign of her—or any other visitors, come to that.'

Kate smiled. 'Well, if you're worried, or think he's not making progress over the next couple of days, call the surgery and I'll come straight out.'

Pat Matthews looked at her. 'What are his chances of coming through this?'

'I'd be lying if I said I could guarantee it. A lot depends on Ed himself. He's always been pretty strong, I gather.' She snapped the locks on her briefcase. 'The question is whether he *wants* to get through it. The critical factor is the next couple of days. If we can get over that, I'd say we can be a bit more positive about the future.'

It was almost dark when she and Sam finally hurried out into the cool of the evening.

Out of habit Kate moved wearily towards the driver's door. She suddenly remembered that Sam had the keys and turned, almost colliding with his solid, muscular frame.

Flustered, she gave a slight laugh. 'Sorry, it's been a long day.'

'And then some.' He smiled, then stared down at her. She heard him draw in a breath and, before she knew what was happening, his mouth came down to brush against hers. She found herself holding her breath as a strange new sense of awareness brought faint colour to her cheeks.

'I'm glad you were with me.'

'I didn't do anything.'

'You were there when it mattered. Thanks.'

'Any time.'

She climbed into the passenger seat, glad of the early darkness and a breeze that cooled her cheeks. Leaning her head back against the seat, Kate closed her eyes, feeling suddenly very weary.

After she'd given him directions to her cottage Sam

drove in silence for a while and she was glad. Her head seemed to be spinning. Lack of food, probably, she silently chided herself.

But it was more than that, she knew. It was a combination of things and concern for Ed Bristow was only part of it. There was also a sudden and very disturbing awareness of her own increasing vulnerability where Sam was concerned. It came as a shock to realise that, if she wasn't very careful, she could become seriously attracted to this man.

In the fading light she watched as he drove. She was beginning to realise that there were hidden depths to Sam Slater. She had been moved by his patience, not only with Ed Bristow but with other patients, too.

He didn't say much, she thought, but he had a way of inspiring confidence. The sort of man you'd trust, she thought drowsily. The sort of man who could persuade patients to place their lives in his hands. Such strong, capable hands.

Kate blinked hard suddenly as memories of the forcefulness with which he'd drawn her towards him and kissed her sent an involuntary flush of anticipation running through her, and she had to drag herself back to reality, stifling a sigh.

'Tired?' Sam turned his head to glance in her direction.

She nodded, reluctant to open her eyes but suddenly, illogically, very glad to have him there.

'You did the right thing, you know.'

Kate sighed. 'That's the problem. I feel as though the decision was taken out of my hands. I wasn't given a choice. Should I have been stronger?'

As they reached the cottage he brought the car to a halt, cutting the ignition but making no attempt to get out. 'You did what was best for the patient, Kate. He's an old man. He's ill and scared. In my experience, sometimes you have to go along with what the patient wants rather than what your instincts tell you. Chances are, even if you'd persuaded him to go to hospital, he'd simply have given up. I've seen it happen.'

'I know that what you're saying makes sense, but that doesn't make it any easier, does it?' She looked at him. 'Ever since I've known Ed he's always been such a strong character, so active, so independent. It came as a shock, seeing him like that, that's all.'

Sam frowned. 'Right now he's just a sick old man, Kate.' He was so close that his arm, along the seat behind her, brushed against her hair.

'I know.'

'You couldn't have done more.'

She sighed. 'I know that, too. But he looked so small, so vulnerable...'

'Don't do this to yourself, Kate. You've nothing to feel guilty about.' Sam's hand was on her shoulder, gently forcing her to look at him. He caught the slight tremor of her lips, the glint of tears in her eyes. She heard him swear softly, then she was fumbling frantically with the doorhandle and climbing out.

He was beside her before she could gather up her things, holding her when she would have broken away.

'Kate, would it help to talk?'

'I don't think so.' She sniffed hard. 'I know I'm not being logical. Ed is a patient and I know we're not supposed to become emotionally involved. It came as a shock, that's all, to see how much he'd changed.' She gave a slight laugh. 'Come rain or snow, it was nothing to see Ed striding out along the lanes with his dog beside him. Now even the dog has gone.'

Sam's gaze narrowed. 'It had to happen sooner or later. You must have seen it with other patients?'

'Yes, of course I have. I just—' She broke off as, from inside the cottage, the phone began to ring. 'I'll have to answer that, it might be urgent.' With a small sigh of exasperation she fumbled in her bag for the key, inserted it in the lock and, without pausing to close the door, hurried to answer it.

'Yes, Dr Dawson speaking. Oh, hello, Mr Lawrence. Yes, I saw your wife and little boy at the surgery yesterday. Is she still worried? Yes, I remember it was quite a nasty ear infection. Unfortunately the antibiotics do take some time to start working so Daniel is probably going to feel quite poorly for a day or so.'

Outside, she heard the car engine start up and glanced through the window in time to see it drive away. For the first time in a long time, a sudden feeling of loneliness swept over her. She felt a sense of disappointment run through her.

So what did you expect? she chided herself. Did you think he was going to come after you? Why would he? Sam has other fish to fry. And even if he had. What then? You don't need this kind of complication in your life, remember?

Swallowing hard on the tightness in her throat, she forced herself to concentrate. 'Yes, Mr Lawrence, I'm still here. No. No, I agree, it is very distressing. What I suggest is that you give him a dose of Calpol and repeat it in four hours if he's awake. But I'm sure you'll find it helps. No, not at all. Certainly give me a call again if you're worried. Any time.'

She replaced the receiver and stood for a few seconds, gazing into the semi-darkness of the room. Her head ached. Sighing, she straightened up, tossed her jacket onto a chair and made her way into the kitchen. What you need, she told herself briskly, is a cup of coffee, a hot shower and an early night.

The door opened before she could reach it and she came to an abrupt halt, blinking as the glare of light hit her. She gasped as Sam held out a cup.

'I thought you might be glad of this. And these are yours.' He dropped the car keys into her hand. 'I parked it in the garage.'

She stared at him, suddenly not knowing what to say, confused by a welter of emotions she was trying desperately not to acknowledge.

'I—I thought you'd gone.'

'Did you really imagine I'd just walk away, Kate?' He spooned sugar into her cup and she stared at him, wishing she hadn't as her eyes encountered his mouth, firm and sensual and far too much of a threat to her peace of mind.

She bit at her lip. 'It's getting late.'

'So it is,' he said softly. He drained his own coffee and set the cup on the table. 'I meant what I said—if you want to talk.'

She shook her head and gave a slight laugh. 'No. You were right. I did what I could. I'm just tired, that's all.'

'So why are you letting it get to you?' Sam's hand caught at her arm, sending a mass of ill-timed signals flaring through her. Her head rose and she felt the full weight of those blue eyes studying her. 'We've all done it, Kate, let ourselves get involved whether we should or not. We know it's not professional but we're only human. It's nothing to be ashamed of.'

She swallowed hard. 'He shouldn't be alone.'

'No, you're right, he shouldn't. But that isn't your fault.'

'So you're saying that's it? There's nothing we can do so let's forget it? End of story?'

'That's not what I'm saying at all.' A nerve pulsed in

his jaw as he drew her slowly towards him. 'Hey, come on. You said yourself, Ed's a tough old character. He's not going to quit, not without a fight. The antibiotics may do the trick.'

Her breath snagged in her throat as his hands cupped her face, bringing her so close that her nostrils were invaded by the clean, musky smell of him. He was making her feel alive in a way she never had before, not even with Colin.

The sensual mouth was just a breath away. Shock briefly widened her eyes as he bent his head slowly to brush his lips against her mouth. The contact sent a rush of desire running through her. It was crazy but she didn't seem to be able to prevent it.

Kate stood, shocked by the power of the sensations that coursed through her. His warm breath fanned her cheek as he stared down at her. She felt his gaze sweep over the creamy translucence of her skin and she began to tremble as his head lifted and for a moment he looked into her face.

This shouldn't be happening, she told herself as desire threatened to flare out of control. She made a soft sound of protest, trying to turn her head away, but Sam wouldn't allow it, pulling her closer still, if that were possible, until she couldn't help being aware of the taut maleness of his body.

'What are you so afraid of, Kate?' he rasped. 'You must know I'd never hurt you.'

Not intentionally, maybe, the thought hovered. She was aware of his mouth, above her own, before it descended again, brushing aside her denial as she clung to the fading remnants of her resistance.

His lips moved teasingly against her mouth, her throat and her eyes. Then, to her everlasting shame, she stopped struggling as a totally new sensation coursed through her, so breathtakingly exquisite that, almost against her will, she found herself responding.

She didn't move. Her limbs felt strangely weak as she looked at him, her eyes focusing with renewed clarity on his tautly honed features. He drew her towards him, his hand moving behind her head to capture the slender column of her neck and tangle with the silky mass of hair at her nape.

Confused, she lifted her face to his. She could hear the muted sound of her own heartbeat as his mouth claimed hers once more, cutting off the protest that rose, fleetingly, to her lips.

It would be so easy to let go, to allow herself to be caught up in what was happening to her. But she had already been down that road before and it had led nowhere, except to disaster. A sense of panic suddenly overwhelmed her.

'Please, no,' Kate breathed raggedly, her hand pressing against him as she tried to break free.

She felt him tense. He stared at her, then abruptly he let her go.

'You're right. It's late. I think it's time I left, before I do something we might both regret,' Sam rasped. 'I have to walk back to the surgery to pick up my car.'

She stared after him and heard the door close before she finally headed for the kitchen to make herself a fresh cup of coffee.

Stirring in sugar lethargically, she told herself there wasn't any reason why she should let him affect her like this, and yet it seemed to happen, that feeling that the moment Sam walked into view he presented some kind of threat.

This is ridiculous, she thought, carrying her cup into the

kitchen where she rinsed it with far more vigour than it warranted.

She had her life all neatly mapped out and it didn't include getting involved, especially with a man like Sam Slater. Getting involved made you vulnerable, and she had no intention of going down that particular path again, thank you very much.

That was easy to say. What she had failed to take into account had been a man like Sam, but at least now she recognised the danger and could be on her guard.

CHAPTER FIVE

Getting out of a warm bed in the middle of the night definitely didn't get any easier, Kate decided.

A blustery wind hurled the remaining leaves from the trees as she made her way quickly to her car and hunted for her keys, wryly acknowledging that this was one aspect of the job she had never quite got used to. And why was it always on the coldest, darkest night?

Not that she had been asleep. Juggling her keys, she finally managed to unlock the car door and tossed her briefcase onto the passenger seat.

She had tried putting her restlessness down to the fact that she had skipped supper, having felt too tired to cook a meal, but knew it was far more to do with a kiss.

For the past few days, whenever their paths had crossed Sam had treated her with nothing more than cool familiarity and, perversely, she felt cheated. She'd thought it was what she wanted, but now she wasn't so sure. She felt bewildered by the conflicting emotions his behaviour had stirred in her.

Stifling a yawn, Kate brought the car to a halt outside the Mitchells' house some ten minutes later, and reached for her briefcase. The door opened as she made her way along the path.

'Oh, Doctor, I'm so glad to see you.' Seventy-five-year-old George Mitchell ushered her into the house. He looked anxious and pale. 'Molly's in the sitting room on the sofa. I didn't know whether I should move her.'

'You did the right thing, leaving her where she is.' Kate was quick to offer the reassurance as she followed the man into the warm sitting room where his wife lay on the sofa, her head resting against a pillow.

Putting her briefcase down, Kate quickly knelt beside the woman whose eyes were closed. Her skin was ashen and clammy and there was a blueness around her lips. Kate's fingers automatically sought for a pulse. It was irregular.

George Mitchell gazed anxiously down at his wife. 'I didn't know what to do for the best. I made her a cup of tea but she couldn't drink it.'

'You did just fine, Mr Mitchell.' Kate looked up at him and smiled. 'Until you know the cause of the problem it's best just to get help rather than try to deal with it yourself.'

As she spoke she was carrying out a quick but gentle examination. Molly's eyes flickered open. She tried to speak but was too breathless and her hand grasped anxiously at Kate's arm.

'It's all right, Mrs Mitchell.' Kate smiled. 'Just try to relax. We'll soon have you sorted out. Can you tell me if you have any pain anywhere?'

The woman's clenched fist fluttered towards her chest. 'Feels tight. Heavy.'

'Anywhere else? Do you have any pain in your arms or neck?'

The woman nodded weakly. 'Left arm.' Her fingers moved to her jaw. 'And here.'

Molly was showing all the classic signs, Kate recognised with growing concern, of a heart attack. She looked at George. 'You said on the phone that your wife had been vomiting.'

'That's right. We were in bed. She must have got up without waking me. It was only when I heard the crash that I realised something was wrong. I found her lying on the bathroom floor.' Tears filled the man's eyes as he looked at Kate. 'It's not good, is it, Doctor?'

Kate lowered her voice as they moved away from the sofa. 'No, I don't think it is. Your wife is obviously very poorly. At this stage it's impossible to tell how serious it is.'

'Is it a stroke, Doctor?'

'No, I don't think so.' Kate was already reaching for her mobile phone. 'Your wife has had a heart attack, Mr Mitchell.' She saw him shake his head. 'The vomiting, the pain in her arm and chest—they're all typical symptoms, I'm afraid.'

She was already tapping out a number on the phone. 'I'm going to arrange to get her into the local hospital. Depending on how severe the attack is, they may decide they want to move her to a larger, better-equipped facility on the mainland. But for now the priority is to get her to the experts.'

'I want to go with her.'

'Yes, of course. That's not a problem,' Kate said gently. 'It might be a good idea if you were to pack a few things into a bag for her. Just a few toiletries, dressing-gown, slippers—things like that.'

As she replaced the phone in her pocket moments later, she breathed an inward sigh of relief. At least help was on its way.

'Do you have any relatives you can call?' she said. 'Someone who can stay with you for a while?'

George's face clouded with confusion. 'There's my daughter…'

'Why not give her a call? Or would you like me to do it for you?'

'No, I'd best do it. It'll be a bit of a shock. How long do you think she'll be in hospital, Doctor?'

'I really can't say at this stage,' she said gently. 'The best thing now is to get her started on the treatment. They'll be able to give her something to ease the pain, and generally make her more comfortable. Hopefully we'll know more in a couple of days.'

It was another half-hour before she drove back to the cottage where she made herself a hot drink, before finally falling into bed. Exhausted, she pulled the duvet around her and closed her eyes.

She woke two hours later to bright daylight with a splitting headache and the annoying certainty that she had overslept. Consequently she arrived at the surgery breathless and having had no breakfast, as well as being twenty minutes late.

Neither did it help matters when she hurried into Reception to gather up her list of visits for the morning to find Sam already there, grimly contemplating the morning's mail.

His glance skimmed over her as she walked into the small office, his expression a dark frown.

'Good morning,' she said, juggling her briefcase and a batch of cards.

'Is it? I hadn't noticed.' The laconic reply made her pause as she reached across the desk to glance at the diary.

Frowning, she flipped the pages before she looked up at him. 'Well, at least I'm hoping it can't get any worse,' she murmured, wondering what had brought on his black mood and deciding to ignore it. 'I'm sorry I'm late,' she said. 'I was called out in the early hours of the morning—'

'I thought I heard a car drive through the village,' he said evenly 'around four-thirty. It's unusual to hear traffic at that hour.'

'Well, I'm very sorry, Doctor. I'll do my very best not to disturb you in future.'

A muscle worked in his jaw and Kate felt an unexpected

tremor run through her as he looked down at her with brooding eyes.

'It does seem to be becoming something of a habit, doesn't it?' he remarked, a cool grimace twisting his mouth.

She glared intently at the attractive planes of his face, looking for some sign of amusement at her expense. His mouth was nerve-shatteringly sensual.

She drew herself up sharply. 'It was dawn before I fell into bed again. I'm beginning to think it was a mistake. I feel worse than if I'd stayed awake.'

'I know the feeling, but it's hard to rationalise when all you want to do is sleep. So, what was the emergency?'

She ran a hand wearily through her hair. 'George Mitchell called, obviously in a bit of a state. His wife had collapsed.'

Sam frowned. 'When you say "collapsed", what do you mean exactly?'

Kate looked at him sharply. Was he actually questioning her judgement? 'I was using George's words. He actually found her lying on the bathroom floor. It was pretty obvious that she'd suffered a severe heart attack.'

She frowned. 'Look, I don't know why I'm bothering to explain all this. Yes, all right, so I was a few minutes late, but I'll make sure the patients don't lose out. It's hardly my fault if you're having a lousy morning.'

She saw the muscle tighten in his jaw and wondered again what had brought on his unaccustomed mood.

His own glance moved glitteringly over her, making a swift assessment of the pale-coloured shirt, which clung gently to her feminine curves, and dropping to sweep over the neatly tailored, calf-length skirt which emphasised the slender curves of her waist and hips. She had dressed in a hurry, for practicality, but under that raking glance she felt her colour rise.

Crisply, she said, 'I hope you're not going to snarl at the staff like a bear with a sore head, otherwise we could have a mutiny on our hands.'

'I wasn't aware that was what I was doing.' He frowned. 'I certainly hadn't intended to question your actions.'

'Well, I'm glad to hear it.' Returning his stare, her gaze ran the length of him, taking in the clean lines of his expensively tailored suit. His dark, casually styled hair looked as if it had been recently trimmed.

She had to resist an almost compulsive yet totally illogical desire to run her fingers through its silky darkness and disturb its neatness.

She swallowed hard and glanced at her watch. 'I'd better make a start. Hopefully, the day can only get better.' She walked through the small office to collect a pack of spatulas from the supply cupboard.

'Kate, wait.'

Sam followed her, pausing in the doorway. 'You're right. I'm sorry. I had no right taking my mood out on you.' His mouth made a wry curve. 'I'd only just walked in the door when a rep turned up without an appointment, expecting to be seen before surgery. Like a fool, I agreed to give him five minutes. It was half an hour before I could get rid of him. I wasn't happy, I can tell you.'

She gave a slight smile. 'No, I don't imagine you were.' She almost found it in her to feel sympathy for the man. 'Did he get the message?'

'Oh, I think so. I made it quite clear that either he makes a proper appointment in future, or he waits until I've seen my last patient. I'm certainly not about to start prescribing drugs I know nothing about, and I'm not likely to be persuaded of their merits by a heated discussion early in the morning before I've had at least two cups of coffee.'

Kate grinned. 'I take it, then, that we can safely say his

day didn't get off to a brilliant start either?' Her glance went to the vacuum jug of coffee on a small side table, and she put her briefcase down.

'Look, I don't know about you, but I could do with a cup of coffee before I start. How about you?'

Frowning, he looked at his watch. 'Oh, what the heck. Why not? It sounds like a great idea to me.'

Kate poured two cups of coffee, adding sugar to her own cup while he glanced through the case notes he was holding.

'Milk?' He nodded absently and she queried softly, 'Is something wrong?'

He dropped the cards on to the table as she proffered a cup. 'I'm not sure. I hope not.'

'Will it help to talk about it?' She watched as he spooned sugar into the coffee.

'A patient came to see me a couple of weeks ago. A sixty-two-year-old man,' Sam stirred his coffee, gazing into the dark, steaming liquid. 'It took a while and some considerable persuasion before I could finally get him to tell me what the problem was. He talked about 'a spot of bother and a bit of trouble with the water works'. He also complained of a burning sensation in his lower abdomen when he passed urine.'

'Did he have a history of urinary infections?'

'No.' Sam shook his head. 'That was my first thought, especially when he said he seemed constantly to be "on the run", as he put it.'

'Did he produce a urine specimen?'

'Yes. I tested it and it showed some evidence of an infection. Naturally I prescribed a course of antibiotics.'

Kate looked at him as she sipped her coffee. 'And you examined him?'

He nodded. 'And as a result I arranged for him to have tests at the hospital.'

'Sam,' she said quietly, 'are you saying what I think you're trying to say?'

He put his cup down to hunt for the case notes again. 'I had the results of the tests through this morning.' He sounded quietly angry. 'It's pretty much what I suspected. Prostate cancer.'

'Operable?'

His mouth tightened. 'It's too far advanced. He's coming in to see me this morning. I have to break the news.' He ran a hand wearily through his hair. 'I feel so bloody useless.'

She gave a slight laugh. 'Hey, come on, Sam. It's not your fault.'

'I know that, but it doesn't make it any easier. If only he'd come to see me earlier. He'd had these symptoms for months—kept telling himself that if he ignored them they'd go away.'

'But, of course, they didn't,' Kate said quietly.

Sam grimaced. '*Why?* What does it take to make men acknowledge that they have a problem? What makes them bury their heads in the sand?'

'Fear? Embarrassment?' Kate frowned. She could see now why he had been so testy when she had walked into Reception. Clearly she wasn't the only one to find there were some aspects of this job that were unpleasant.

'It wasn't your fault, Sam,' she reminded him gently. 'You did what you could. It's attitudes that need to be changed and that's not going to happen overnight. Stop blaming yourself.'

She put her cup down and reached for her briefcase. 'Look, I'm really sorry, but I do have to make a start.'

Sam looked at his own watch and followed her to the

door. 'I think I'd like to go back to bed and start today all over again.' He pulled open the door and walked out of Reception. In a moment or two a buzzer sounded and Lucy called for the first patient to go along to his room.

It turned out to be a busy morning, with the usual crop of ailments. An hour and a half later Kate was beginning to look forward to a break.

Maggie Hughes hovered uncertainly in the open doorway. 'Hi, Kate. Look, I'm sorry about this. I don't have an appointment but Lucy said she'd tack me on at the end of your list. I can always come back…'

Kate was instantly on her feet. 'Maggie! No, don't you dare go away. It's lovely to see you.' Smiling, she gestured her friend towards the chair. 'Take a seat. Tell me what I can do for you. Or is this a social visit?'

'Actually, no.' Maggie bit at her lip. At thirty-two she was slim, dark-haired and attractive. She sighed and unbuttoned her jacket. 'I took the day off from the office. Phil doesn't know I'm here.' She glanced up and Kate noted the pallor in her cheeks. 'Well, there was no reason to tell him, really. I'm probably wasting your time.'

'Well, let's hope so.' Kate smiled. 'How is Phil, anyway? It's been ages since we last got together.'

'Oh, he's fine. Working hard as usual.'

'Look, I'm due a coffee-break. Would you like some?'

'No, thanks.' Maggie shuddered. Her gaze met Kate's and fell away again. 'To tell you the truth, I haven't been feeling too well for a while.'

Kate frowned. 'When you say "a while", how long, exactly?'

'Oh, three, four weeks or so.'

'Why on earth didn't you come to see me?'

Maggie shrugged, brushing a hand through her hair. 'Well, it's nothing specific really. That's the trouble, I'm beginning to think it's all psychological—you know, to cover a guilt complex or something.'

Kate laughed. 'And why should you feel guilty?'

Maggie sighed. 'I suppose because things haven't been too good between me and Phil for a while. We seem to argue all the time. You know how it is. He thinks I should give up my job. He knows it's been getting to me a bit lately. We have been busy—more so since the take-over. But I enjoy my work.' Her mouth formed a wry grin. 'It's probably indigestion.'

'If it is then it's a little prolonged.' Kate smiled easily. 'Either way, it's troubling you enough to bring you here, so let's see if we can sort things out. Suppose you start by telling me what sort of symptoms you're getting.'

'It's all a bit vague.' Maggie made a dismissive gesture with her hand. 'Like I said, it's nothing I can really put my finger on. Headaches, dizziness, feeling ridiculously weepy for no obvious reason.'

'How about your appetite?'

There was a moment's hesitation. 'Not so good.'

'A feeling of constantly needing to spend a penny?'

Maggie laughed. 'It's probably the amount of coffee I've been drinking.'

Kate sat back in her chair. 'You're sure you've only noticed the symptoms fairly recently?'

'Well, now that you mention it, no, I'm not absolutely certain. I've been so busy at work.' She frowned. 'There's a possibility I might be in line for a promotion and I'm not sure how Phil will take the news.'

'Is it what you want?'

'I thought so.' Maggie sighed. 'I don't mind extra responsibility. Oh, you know how it is. I love what I do, but I'm always conscious that I'm not getting any younger.'

She gave a slight laugh. 'It's hardly surprising that I get the odd dose of heartburn.'

Kate leaned forward. 'So, is it indigestion or heartburn or nausea?'

Maggie stared at her for a moment. 'Well, I suppose it's all three.'

'Ah!' Kate toyed with a pen on her desk. 'Look, to begin with I'd like to give you a general check-up. Did you by any chance bring a urine specimen with you?'

Maggie produced a small bottle from her bag. Hesitantly she handed it over as she rose to her feet. 'You think you know what the problem is, don't you?'

Kate dropped the pen onto her desk and raised an eyebrow. 'Don't you?'

'I'm pregnant, aren't I?'

'I'd say it's a pretty safe bet. All the signs are there. Have you done a pregnancy test?'

'No.' Maggie gave a short laugh. 'I'm still not really sure I want to know.'

Kate sat back in her chair. 'It's probably too early for me to be able to tell from an examination, but I can do a test for you.'

'And when will I know?'

'I'll probably have the results within twenty-four hours. In the meantime, why don't I give you that check-up? Let's start with your blood pressure and then you can pop onto the scales and we'll weigh you.'

Ten minutes later, the examination completed, Kate studied her friend. 'Well, you're in pretty good shape.'

The other woman gave a wry smile. 'Not for long, though, am I? If you're right.'

'I'm as sure as I can be that you're in the early stages of pregnancy.' Having washed her hands, Kate returned to her seat at the desk. 'The question is, how do you feel about it?'

'Well, I'd begun to suspect anyway, so it's not a complete surprise. Still, it'll take a bit of getting used to.'

'I take it it wasn't planned?'

Maggie gave a short laugh. 'You could say. I forgot to take my Pill. I had to go away for a couple of days on company business. Phil came with me. We all met up with our spouses and had a few drinks in the evening…'

Kate grinned. 'I can imagine.'

Maggie toyed with the strap of her handbag. 'Actually, now that I know, so to speak, I'm beginning to quite like the idea of having a baby. I'd always told myself it was a decision I could postpone. I was doing a job I enjoyed and getting paid very nicely, thank you. There didn't seem any reason to give it all up.'

She frowned. 'I knew Phil wanted a baby, of course, but I kept telling myself there was plenty of time for that sort of thing later.'

'After the promotion?'

Maggie looked up with a ghost of a smile. 'It would have been quite something, you know? The company's been expanding. There aren't many female heads of department.'

'You can always go back to work—after the baby is born.'

'Yes, I suppose I can. Though I'm not sure I'll want to. If I'm going to have this baby I want to enjoy it.' She gave a slight smile. 'If I'm honest, I probably didn't stand much of a chance of getting the promotion anyway. Some of the other candidates were more experienced. It was a nice idea, though, while it lasted.'

'I imagine Phil will be delighted about the baby.'

'Oh, he'll have the champagne on ice within five minutes of me breaking the news.' Maggie's face clouded. 'I think

I'll wait for official confirmation of the test first. It will give me time to adjust properly to the idea myself. I'm not ready to be smothered, or treated like a mother-to-be yet.'

'That's perfectly understandable.' Kate smiled as Maggie rose to her feet. 'Why not give me a call some time tomorrow? I should have the results by then.'

'I'll do that,' Maggie confirmed smilingly, as she walked to the door.

Kate stood in the corridor, watching Maggie walk away, and was musing gently to herself on the way someone's life could be so utterly changed in so short a space of time when Jill came hurrying towards her.

'Oh, Kate, thank heavens I caught you. I was afraid you might have left to do your visits. I've just had a call from Mrs Reynolds.' Her expression was anxious and Kate stiffened involuntarily.

'Sally?'

'She sounds really worried about young Jessica. Apparently she's been complaining of a really bad headache.'

Kate frowned. 'Jess is only three, but she's usually such a lively little thing.' She glanced at her watch. 'I'll give Sally a call now.'

At the reception desk she dialled her friend's number. 'Hello, Sally? Yes, it's Kate.'

'Oh, Kate, thank heavens. I'm so sorry to bother you, but I'm worried about Jess. She woke up this morning complaining that her head hurt.'

'Have you given her a dose of Calpol?'

'Yes, but if anything I'd say her temperature is up slightly.'

'Has she been sick?'

'Yes, once. I don't like to bother you but I've never seen her quite so poorly.'

Kate was vaguely aware of Sam coming to stand beside

her at the desk. He signed a couple of letters, handing them over to Jill.

Kate smiled. 'You did absolutely the right thing. It's probably nothing serious. You know what children are—up one minute, down the next. Has she complained of any other aches and pains?'

'She doesn't seem to like the light. She says it hurts her eyes.'

Kate frowned, experiencing her first real pang of alarm. 'Look, I've just finished surgery here. How about if I pop over now and take a look at her?'

'Would you?' There was an audible sigh of relief from the other end of the phone. 'I'm sorry to panic but—'

'I'll be with you in ten minutes.' Replacing the phone, Kate reached for her briefcase.

'Problem?'

She turned to look at Sam. 'A friend of mine. Her little girl is poorly.' Kate couldn't get rid of the sudden tight feeling in her chest. 'She's complaining of headaches and sensitivity to light. Her temperature is up.'

Sam frowned. 'And you're immediately thinking meningitis?'

Kate flicked him a glance. The fact that he had put a name to it somehow only seemed to reinforce her fears. 'Jess is my god-daughter and Sally is my friend,' she said tightly. 'She isn't the hysterical type. If she's worried it's because she has reason.'

'What do you want me to do about Mr Brooks, Kate?' Jill held up a buff folder. 'I said we'd try and get someone out to see him this morning.'

'Damn! I'd forgotten all about him.'

'It's no problem. I'll take it,' Sam said evenly. He slung his jacket over his shoulder and reached out to take the card. He nodded in the direction of the door. 'You go and see your friend.'

Kate swallowed hard. 'Are you sure you don't mind?'

'Like I said, it's no problem. Just go. I'll cover any calls this end. Oh, and best of luck.'

Ten minutes later she pulled up at the Reynolds house, and was met by Sally.

'Where's Jess?'

'Upstairs.' Sally was already leading the way. 'She seems very sleepy and still says her head hurts. I've closed the curtains so that the light doesn't disturb her.'

Jess was lying on the bed. Her eyes were closed and her small face was flushed. Kate put her briefcase down, slipped off her jacket and sat beside her.

Fretfully the child turned her head and whimpered softly.

Looking at her, Kate brushed a finger gently against the three-year-old's cheek. 'Hello, poppet, Mummy tells me you're not feeling well. Can you tell me where it hurts?'

A small, plump hand wavered in the direction of her forehead. Resting a hand gently against the child's cheek, Kate could feel that she had a temperature.

Glancing over her shoulder, she said quietly, 'How long did you say she's been complaining of the headache?'

'She first mentioned it a couple of days ago when I picked her up from the nursery. I didn't worry about it too much because she seemed fine the following morning.'

Kate nodded and reached into her briefcase for an auroscope. 'I just want to take a look in your ears, Jess. I promise it won't hurt.'

Sally watched anxiously as Kate carried out a brief examination.

'Well, they seem clear. There's no sign of any infection. Did you say she's been sick?'

'Just once.'

'What about her appetite?'

'Practically non-existent.'

'I'll just listen to her chest, although there aren't any obvious signs of an infection.' After a few seconds she smiled and patted the child's hand. 'All right, Jess, that bit is all finished. Well, her chest is clear, too. What about her neck? Has she complained of any pain or stiffness?'

Gently she examined the child's neck and ran her fingers over the area around the bridge of her nose and eyes.

Sally bit at her lower lip. 'Jess did say her neck was hurting, and she didn't seem to want to move her head too much.' She looked anxiously at Kate. 'It's not...meningitis, is it?' She reached out for the child's small hand. 'I wasn't sure if I should have called the hospital.' Her voice held a note of panic. 'I knew I should have done something sooner.'

'Sally, I'm as sure as I can be that it's not meningitis.'

'Oh, thank God. So what do you think it is?' She lowered her voice as they moved away from the bed. 'Jess isn't a child who lies around. She's usually playing with her friends and she loves the nursery. She wouldn't miss it. I've never seen her like this before and I'm scared.'

Kate smiled sympathetically. 'I'm always more concerned when a child is unusually quiet than if it's making a lot of noise. In Jess's case, I think she has a fairly nasty sinus infection.'

'Sinus!' Sally gave a short laugh of relief.

Kate nodded. 'It would account for the headache. She probably doesn't notice it too much first thing in the morning, but it builds up during the day. It explains the temperature and the neck stiffness, too. She doesn't want to move her head too much because it hurts.'

Sally gave a deep sigh of relief. 'Oh, Kate, I've been so worried. I was so sure it was meningitis.'

'I can understand why. But you did absolutely the right thing in calling me.' Kate smiled. 'I'm going to give you a prescription for an antibiotic. It's in liquid form and quite pleasant so you shouldn't have any problems getting Jess to take it. It is important that she completes the course. Meanwhile, give her Calpol to help relieve the pain and I'm sure you'll soon see a definite improvement.'

'I don't know how to thank you...'

'Sally, there's no need. It's what I'm here for and Jess is very special to me, you know that.'

'Well, as long as you know that I'm grateful.' Sally's anxieties had clearly been alleviated, simply by knowing the cause of her daughter's distress. 'Will you stay and have a cup of tea? It seems ages since we had a long chat.'

'I'd love to.' Kate looked at her watch and pulled a wry face. 'But I'd better not. It's my afternoon off and I've a mountain of chores I've been putting off. Perhaps we can get together some time soon?'

It was ludicrous, she thought as she drove in surprisingly warm afternoon sunshine back to the cottage later, to find herself actually resenting a whole afternoon of unplanned idleness. It was a luxury she'd been promising herself for ages, but now that the miracle had happened, somehow the prospect of spending several hours on household chores had definitely lost its charm.

Sitting in the neat little kitchen, sipping at her coffee, she was trying to summon enough enthusiasm to tackle cleaning the cooker when a rap on the door made a sharp intrusion into her thoughts, and she was still frowning as she went to open it.

'Hello, Kate.'

'Sam!' He had changed out of his formal suit and was casually dressed in denim jeans and a black sweatshirt. Her heart gave a tiny, unaccustomed jerk. 'Is...is there a problem?'

'Not that I'm aware of.' His mouth curved in a smile. 'Why? Does there have to be for me to say hello?'

'No, I suppose not.' She half turned away in an attempt to hide the sudden rise of colour in her cheeks. 'I just wasn't expecting you, that's all. You'd...better come in. The kitchen is through here. Not very large, I'm afraid.' He ducked to avoid the low ceilings.

Kate gazed at him and wished she hadn't. A six-foot-and-then-some man in a tiny kitchen could be a problem in more ways than one!

She averted her eyes and flipped the switch on the electric kettle. 'Coffee? I was just having some.'

He looked at the solitary cup on the table and frowned. 'So I see. I take it this is lunch?'

'It's as far as I got.'

'As a matter of fact, I haven't eaten either. I was wondering, would you like to go for a walk? I found a rather nice little pub. Perhaps we could go for a drink and something to eat? It's down in the bay—a nice place, especially when all the tourists have gone.' He looked at her. 'Unless you've something else arranged...?'

'No.' She shook her head, dry-mouthed, and thought dazedly how startlingly blue his eyes were. 'I...I'd love to go for a walk.'

'You might need a jacket. It gets chilly once the sun starts to go down.'

The tide was on the turn and the small craft were bobbing in the water as they made their way to the pub, moving gratefully into its welcoming interior.

It was quiet, with just a few locals at the bar.

'How about this table by the window? I'll get the drinks while you study the menu.'

She slid into the seat and eased a stray wisp of hair behind her ear. 'This is nice,' she said, as he returned to the table, carrying two large glasses.

'I found it quite by chance one day. Here you go. The local nectar.' He held out a tall, frosted glass to her. 'Very cold and delicious.'

'Thanks.' She swallowed greedily, surprised to discover just how thirsty she was.

'And how about food?'

She scanned the menu and shook her head in confusion. 'I can't decide. It all sounds wonderful. You choose.'

He grinned. 'You're sure you want me to surprise you?'

Well, wasn't he always doing that anyway? she thought.

Their food arrived a surprisingly short time after they'd ordered, and they ate surrounded by the gentle hubbub of conversation around them.

She hadn't imagined she would be hungry, but when it came to it she found she was, in fact, ravenous.

Sam grinned. 'I take it that was good?'

Colour flared in her cheeks. 'It certainly beats the cheese sandwich I was eventually going to get round to.'

'That's what I thought.' Sam cast a considering glance over her as he drained the last of his drink. 'How's the little girl? Jess, did you say her name was? You were worried.'

'Yes, I was.' She frowned as she toyed with her glass. 'You never know with children, do you? I mean they can be fine one minute and frighteningly poorly the next.'

'You were afraid it might be meningitis.'

'Sally obviously thought it might be, and I don't blame her. The symptoms could have pointed to it.'

'But it wasn't?' he said softly.

Kate put her glass on the table and drew a deep breath. 'No, thank God. Oh, Jess is certainly quite poorly and not very happy, poor little thing. But I'm as sure as I can be that she's got a sinus infection. I've prescribed some antibiotics so she should be fine in a few days.'

He grimaced ruefully. 'But it doesn't lessen the feelings of panic her mother must have gone through, does it?'

'No, it doesn't.' Kate glanced at him, touched by his perceptiveness. 'Is that... Is that why you came to the cottage? To find out how Jess was?'

'I knew you were worried. It occurred to me that you probably hadn't eaten.' He shot her a sideways look that was suddenly laced with humour. 'Neither had I, and it seemed like a perfect opportunity to escape for a while.' He put his glass down. 'Shall we go?'

She nodded distractedly, suddenly reluctant to move. The touch of his hand, the palm flat, the long fingers resting lightly against the thin cotton of her blouse, was having an unnerving effect on her senses. To him, it was just a natural gesture, but it had the effect of sending Kate's blood pressure soaring to danger level.

It was crazy. What was the matter with her? Why was it that with every new thing she learned about Sam, she became more and more vulnerable to his every move?

Breathing deeply, she tried to shake away the thought. They had left the pub behind, and now she could see that they were headed along a narrow pathway across the dunes.

'This isn't the way back,' she said, puzzled.

'I promised you a walk. This is it. Besides, it will be cooler by the water.'

'But—'

'Come on, it's this way.'

He took her hand, helping her along the narrow coastal path towards a group of gnarled trees.

Pausing for a moment, she shaded her eyes and gazed out at the small harbour below, experiencing the same delight at the scene now as she had when she had first arrived on Hellensey.

A few hardy tourists had stayed on, enjoying the remnants of a mild autumn before winter set in. That was one of the things she loved about the island. It had something to offer at any time of year.

Beyond the sea wall, the tide was out, leaving a few small craft moored on the sand-bed in the harbour. On the far side of the cove the weak afternoon sun cut a golden trail across the water as a succession of small boats moved out of the harbour in search of deeper fishing grounds.

Kate stood still, absorbing the beauty of the scene. 'This is so beautiful,' she whispered. 'I never get tired of looking at it. Even in the winter—*especially* in the winter—it can be awe-inspiring.'

'I know what you mean,' Sam said quietly.

Kate stared in fascination as seagulls hovered noisily at the water's edge. It was a long time since she had been up here.

In the beginning it had almost become something of a retreat, a place to go, to be alone. Was that what had brought Sam here? she wondered. He said he had put the past behind him, but was it ever that easy? Or maybe it was someone else he was missing. Someone who had given him a new purpose in life? A reason to go on living?

She stirred, feeling suddenly restless. A cool breeze blew a wisp of hair against her cheek as she moved to sit on a low outcrop of rock.

Leaning back, she continued to survey the scene, her senses gradually lulled by the sun's warmth. Her eyelids became heavy and she felt her body relax, filled with a sense of languor. Only the hum of insects and the soft wash of the distant waves disturbed the air.

'It's so peaceful,' she breathed, 'and I can't believe it's so warm. This morning I thought winter had arrived.'

'It's good to escape every now and then.' Sam spoke softly and she opened her eyes to find his blue gaze dwelling on her.

Suddenly she remembered the few moments she had spent in his arms and she looked away, a faint flush running along her cheek-bones.

'Oh, look,' she said, seeking a distraction. 'There's a cormorant, sunning itself on one of the rocks. I love the way they spread their wings to dry their feathers.'

'I expect he's done a hard day's fishing.' Sam joined her, sitting on the rock. 'I'm glad I found this place.'

Lazily, she lifted a brow. 'It's a bit different to Africa.'

His mouth tilted at the corners. 'It certainly is. I seem to recall that the smells out there were slightly more exotic than those of the local fish and chips!'

Kate gave him a playful push, then her mind wandered and she pictured him in that far-off country, away from family and friends, somehow having to come to terms with his grief. Life had to go on, he'd said. She wondered with a sudden and uncharacteristic twist of jealousy about the woman who had made him believe it.

Straightening, she said, 'You'll miss all of this if…when you leave.' She got to her feet and started to ease herself off the rock.

Sam moved to help her, his hands settling with idle possession about her waist, and as his cool glance meshed with hers she knew a profound and utter confusion.

'I'll miss a lot of things,' he said evenly. Her feet made contact with the ground but there was no solidity to it any more.

Sam was supporting her, his fingers warm on the soft flare of her hips, his thumbs spanning the base of her ribcage. She heard his soft intake of breath, then he bent his head towards her, and the touch of his mouth on hers was coaxingly warm and gentle.

His arms folded about her, the kiss deepening, shocking her into a startled response. She felt the softness of her curves crushed against him, felt the hard strength of his body as his palm flattened on the small of her back, urging her closer to him.

He made her feel shockingly alive and experience things in a way that she never had before, not even with Colin. Heat surged through her body, the blood pounding in her ears.

For a wild, lingering moment she was lost in a vortex of powerful sensations, her body alive with heart-racing excitement. The contact sent a new rush of desire running through her. It was crazy, but she didn't seem to be able to prevent it.

Her face lifted to his. She felt him tense, then suddenly he set her free, his breathing harsh as he drew away, leaving her senses reeling in confusion.

She started to protest, then became dizzyingly aware of the elderly couple strolling towards them, a small dog scampering excitedly at their heels.

Only then, as the heated colour flooded into her face was Kate aware of Sam deliberately shielding her from their gaze, giving her time to recover.

She swept a hand through her hair, guessing at how she must look. Her mouth still felt swollen and the buttons of her blouse had somehow come undone.

His glittering gaze narrowed as he looked at her. 'I think it's time I took you home,' he said huskily, as the couple passed them, making their way along the cliff path.

They arrived back at the cottage half an hour later. For the most part they had driven in silence.

Switching off the engine at last, Sam seemed loath to move. Reaching over, he tilted her chin and looked into her eyes. It was all the trigger her senses needed to set her nerve-ends jangling again as for several seconds she was held within the warm circle of his arms, and once again she was totally unprepared for the primitive way in which she seemed to respond to their brief contact.

'It's been a good day,' Sam said softly.

'Yes, I've enjoyed it, too. Would...would you like to come in for a coffee?'

'I'm tempted,' he said huskily, 'but I think we'd better forget the drink.' He draped her jacket round her shoulders, his hands briefly making contact with her flesh.

She glanced anxiously at her watch. 'Yes, of course. I'm sorry. I didn't realise it was so late.'

His gaze narrowed. 'It's not—yet,' he said tautly. 'But I don't think it would be a good idea.'

Kate swallowed hard. 'Yes, well.' She turned, fumbling with the doorhandle. 'I'll say goodnight, then.'

'Kate.'

She turned and he drew her gently towards him. 'Thank you for today.'

Why couldn't he just let her go? She gasped softly as his mouth came down on hers.

'Goodnight, Kate. Sleep tight.'

She stared after him for several seconds, before leaving the car and going inside to finally make herself a fresh cup of coffee. It wasn't as if there was any reason why she should let him affect her like this, she thought as she sipped her coffee, and yet it seemed to happen the moment he came near her.

But it didn't have to be like that, she chided herself. It was a long time since any man had aroused her to a sense of sexual awareness.

A tremor ran through her. She felt both shocked and appalled. What was she doing? How could she forget so easily?

Furiously she put her cup down and went briskly from room to room, plumping cushions with far more vigour than they warranted, until she came to a halt, breathing hard.

This is ridiculous, she told herself, brushing a hand against her eyes. She loved her life as it was, she wasn't going to go through the pain of another relationship—especially with a man like Sam Slater.

CHAPTER SIX

DRIVING to the surgery the following morning, Kate found herself dreading the inevitable meeting with Sam.

She had woken feeling exhausted and hollow-eyed, and as a result of her tossing and turning there were shadows beneath her eyes, and her face, when she looked in the mirror, was so pale that she resorted to a hint of blusher on her cheeks, before making her way with uncharacteristic reluctance to the surgery.

She pulled into the car park just as Sam was getting out of his own car. She sat, purposely foraging in her bag, hoping that he would go in ahead of her, but he turned back to collect a journal he'd left on the seat, and as he straightened up their eyes locked before he slammed the door and came towards her.

Sighing, she climbed out of her car and locked it.

'I'm glad I caught you. I meant to give you this. There's an article about Lyme disease. I thought you might find it interesting.'

'Yes, I will. Thanks.'

He inclined his head in acknowledgement. 'Sleep well?'

A small pulse began to hammer in her throat. 'Like a log, thank you.' She withdrew her hand from his grasp, but not before she had seen his mouth curve in silent laughter.

'I wish I could say the same. I seem to have been tossing and turning all night.'

'Too much caffeine,' she snapped, making her way briskly towards Reception. 'You should try cutting down on the coffee.'

'I'll bear that in mind,' he said gravely, as he held the door open. 'By the way, any news on your heart-attack patient? What was her name?'

'Mitchell. Molly Mitchell. Yes.' Kate nodded. 'As a matter of fact I phoned the hospital last night. She's doing well. She's not out of the woods yet, obviously, but they think she'll be all right.'

'Oh, well, that's good news.'

'Excuse me, Doctor.' A patient wheeling a pushchair came out of the treatment room, apologising as she edged past them in the corridor.

Instinctively, Sam drew Kate aside, his arm round her as, smiling, the woman made her way out.

For several seconds she was held within the warm circle of his arm. His skin smelled faintly of aftershave, and once again she was totally unprepared for the way in which, for those few seconds, she seemed to respond to that brief contact.

She stiffened, half stepping back as her gaze shot upwards into the blue eyes that regarded her with a hint of laughter in them.

Taking several deep breaths, she looked pointedly at her watch and said briskly, 'Yes, well, if you'll excuse me, I do have some work to do.'

In Reception she collect the morning mail and a list of patients' appointments, before making her way to her consulting room.

Shedding her jacket, she checked her appearance as usual in the mirror—fashionable denim skirt and a neat, cap-sleeved T-shirt.

Seating herself at the desk, she switched on the computer, watched the screen flare into life, sighed and pressed the buzzer, summoning her first patient of the day.

An hour and a half later, Lucy tapped at the door and

popped her head round. 'Sorry to bother you, but Mr Jarvis rang to cancel his appointment.'

Washing her hands, Kate returned to her desk and found the appropriate card. 'Right, that's one less to worry about. Did he say why?'

'He says his sore throat seems to have sorted itself out and he's taking paracetamol, which helps.'

Kate frowned. 'I see from his notes that he's taking regular medication to lower his blood pressure. Has he been in to have it checked recently?'

Sue Reynolds, the practice nurse, entered the room and dropped a bundle of cards onto the desk. 'I saw him a couple of weeks ago. He was fine.'

Kate nodded. 'Right, in that case I don't need to see him.' She looked at her watch. 'Does that mean I've finished?'

'Ah, no, sorry. Not quite.' Lucy hunted for a notepad. 'We've had a call from the local primary school. One of the children has had a bit of an accident. The teacher is bringing him to the surgery.'

'Did they say what the problem is?'

'Only that something had fallen on him. I think he had a bump on the head, so I suggested they bring him in for a check-up, just to be on the safe side.'

'He didn't actually lose consciousness?'

'No. I did ask because I thought you'd probably say not to move him if that was the case.'

'Fine.'

Lucy glanced out of the window as a car drew up on the drive. 'Actually, I think that may be them now.'

'Is the treatment room free, do you know?'

'Yes, it is.' Sue nodded. 'I finished my clinic about ten minutes ago, so it's all yours.'

'Better just make sure everything is ready, just in case we have a stitching job on our hands.'

Lucy pulled a face. 'Sooner you than me.'

'Do we know what the child's name is?'

'Yes, it's...Harry Williams. I got his medical notes out for you.'

'Thanks.' Kate glanced at the card and frowned. 'What about his parents? Has anyone informed them?'

'The school managed to contact the mum. She's on her way here now.'

'Right. Bring them through to the treatment room as soon as you're ready.'

The patient, a ginger-haired seven-year-old, was clearly not happy. He clasped a blood-stained hanky to a wound on his forehead. Tears trickled down his cheeks and he used a grubby fist to dash them away.

'Hello, Harry. My goodness! What have you been up to?'

Kate smiled at the harassed-looking teacher. 'Bring him through here and we'll take a look at the damage. Can you hop up onto the couch, Harry? Or do you need a lift?'

'Oh, Harry's an expert at climbing, aren't you, Harry?' Helen Watkins smiled wryly as she ruffled the child's hair. 'He was mountaineering over a stack of chairs when this happened. The children have been warned not to go into the storeroom.'

Kate grinned. 'I see. Well, let's clean this up a bit so that I can take a proper look at the damage. I take it there aren't any other injuries?'

'A bruise on his arm. He got off amazingly lightly, thank goodness. Scared the rest of us to death, mind. There seemed to be an awful lot of blood.'

'There often is with a head wound. Oh, yes.' Kate studied the fairly deep gash just above one eye. 'Well, you certainly made a good job of this, didn't you, young man?'

Harry wasn't fooled by small talk. He sniffed hard. 'I want my mum.'

'She'll be here very soon.' Kate frowned. 'This is quite a nasty cut.' She looked at the teacher. 'You're sure he didn't lose consciousness, not even for a few seconds?'

'Not a chance.' Helen Watkins laughed. 'The whole school heard the noise.'

'Oh, well, that's good. There's always a danger of concussion. We have to check.'

'You're not going to sew it up, are you?' The victim thrust away Kate's hand as she tried to swab away some of the blood from the site of the injury. She glanced at the teacher, who sighed heavily.

'Harry knows all about these things. It runs in the family. His brother James was in my class two years ago. He managed to break his wrist, falling from a tree.' She bit at her lower lip. 'You're *not* going to have to stitch it, are you?'

Kate turned away, reaching for another swab. 'I don't think so. We try not to stitch injuries on children unless it really can't be avoided,' she confided quietly. 'In this case the wound looks nasty but...' She peered more closely. 'Actually, it's quite clean.'

'Oh, thank goodness for that.'

Kate lowered her voice, deliberately moving away from the examination couch. 'Ideally it needs a couple of stitches, but I don't think he's going to let anyone try, and there's no point upsetting him even more than he already is. I think we'll try some steri-strips. They should hold the edges of the skin in place long enough for it to start healing.'

Turning, she smiled. 'So, young man, what are we going to do with you?'

'Put a bandage on it.' One grubby fist kneaded at his eyes.

Kate grinned. 'I'm not sure a bandage would do the trick. But I'm sure we can come up with something to impress your friends.'

'Michael fell over and had a big plaster on his knee.' Harry dashed a hand against his eyes.

'Well I'm sure we can do better than that.' Kate smiled. 'Steri-strips and a large dressing it is.'

Harry held out a dimpled arm and inspected the steadily darkening bruise. 'This hurts, too.'

Helen shook her head. 'I suppose you realise he's going to live on this for the next month.'

Kate chuckled. 'In that case, we'd better make it really impressive, hadn't we?'

A couple of minutes later she had seen her patient out and was washing her hands.

'You did a good job there.' Sam spoke from the doorway. He was carrying his jacket slung over one shoulder, revealing tautly muscled arms and chest beneath a white shirt.

A small pulse began to throb at the base of her throat. 'I didn't see you there.'

'I'm not surprised. You had your hands pretty full.' He stood looking at her. 'I'm glad you had to deal with that and not me. I'm hopeless when it comes to dealing with sick children. They always said it would get easier. It never did—not for me, anyway.'

'I can understand that.' She reached for her jacket. Sam helped her into it, his hands curving round her shoulders.

She drew a shaky breath. 'By the way...' she swallowed hard '...I meant to tell you. The results of Mary Duncan's blood tests came through. You were right. It was Lyme disease.'

'Well, that's great. At least now you can get her started

on the appropriate antibiotics.' He held the door for her as they walked through to Reception.

She forced herself to turn and look at him. 'I really am grateful, Sam.'

'I told you, there's no need. If the result is one happy patient then we're all pleased. Any more news of Ed Bristow?'

'I've spoken to Mrs Matthews. At least he's taking the tablets—so far.'

'At least that's something.'

'I'll keep an eye on him.' She frowned. 'I've made a few enquiries. It seems his wife died a few years ago, following a stroke. There was a daughter.'

'Was?'

'Mmm. From what I can gather, she lived with her family in one of the old cottages down by the harbour. It seems there was some sort of family rift. She moved away and no one seems to have heard from her since.'

Sam frowned. 'It's sad when that sort of thing happens, and so often it's unnecessary. If only people would talk.'

But it wasn't always so easy, was it? Kate thought, as a fleeting memory of her own parents' arguments lashed unbidden into her mind. The endless arguments, the tears. The times she'd lain in bed with the covers pulled over her head to try and shut out the awful sounds.

And then, when she'd grown up and had thought she'd been safe, it had happened all over again. Only this time the arguments had been between herself and Colin.

Her throat tightened as she tried to compose herself. 'I suppose some things just can't be resolved.'

'Maybe not. But that doesn't mean it always has to go wrong, Kate. Sometimes things do work out.'

She nodded perfunctorily, then realised he was staring at her with a look of sympathy and understanding. It didn't help. It reminded her far too vividly of her own vulnerability where this man was concerned. All the more reason to be on her guard.

She gave herself a mental shake. 'I'm going to be late. If I don't make a start on my calls soon I'm never going to get back for evening surgery.'

'Oh, Doctor...' Jill smiled as she came through from the office. 'I'm glad I caught you. Mrs Oliver telephoned to remind us about the forthcoming event.'

Kate's heart sank. 'Oh, no!'

Sam frowned. 'What's the problem?'

'Mrs Oliver. She's chairman—chair*person*—of the local fête committee. She does endless good works.'

'Don't tell me.' He groaned. 'I know the type. I usually manage to avoid them.'

'Well, I've news for you, Dr Slater.' Kate's eyes sparkled with satisfaction as she snapped the locks on her briefcase and headed for the door. 'This is one event you won't be able to avoid.'

'What do you mean?'

'Didn't they tell you?' Her face assumed an innocent expression which didn't fool him for one minute. 'You and I are duty doctors this year.' She darted him a glance and grinned. 'You'll love it.'

'Somehow I doubt that,' he growled as he followed her to the car park. 'Perhaps it will rain, or snow even.'

Kate laughed. 'You should be so lucky.' She wound down her car window and waved as she drove off.

In the event, the day dawned bright and the heat was already beginning to build when Sam arrived to pick Kate up.

Their arrival at the show caused an immediate ripple of

attention. Margaret Oliver came towards them, hooking her hand possessively into Sam's arm.

'Dr Slater and Dr Dawson. I do hope we're not going to keep you too busy today. Things are going so well and we have the perfect day for it, so you must find time to join in with all the activities.'

She beamed at Sam from beneath the brim of her large feathered hat. 'Of course, this is the first time for you, isn't it? Although I say it myself, our little event is very popular.'

'I'm sure it is.' Sam smiled. 'And I can see why.'

'How are you settling in on the island? Do you intend staying with us or is this just a temporary...?'

Caught up in a huddle with the rest of those coerced into offering their services, Kate was unable to catch his reply and bit her lip with frustration as she eased her way out of the crush and headed for the first-aid tent.

After that she was too busy casting a professional eye over the equipment and facilities provided to have time to think too much about Sam.

The event was going well. The local people had turned out in full force, as had outsiders, drawn by what had proved to a popular yearly event.

The weather helped, too, Kate thought, brushing the back of her hand across her forehead as the sun continued to climb in a near-cloudless sky. She was glad she'd chosen to wear the calf-length skirt with the white, cap-sleeved T-shirt, and had tied her hair back in a neat French plait.

For the next couple of hours they were kept busy, mainly with treating minor accidents—cuts and bruises. Kate was just finishing applying a dressing to a bloodied knee when an elderly lady was brought in, supported by a clearly anxious husband.

The woman looked flushed and seemed confused.

'I don't know what's wrong with her, Doctor.' Alfred Baxter took possession of his wife's handbag as Sam led her gently to a chair. 'She just suddenly came over all funny, like.'

'Here we are, Mrs Baxter.' Sam gently helped the woman to sit down. 'I gather you're not feeling too well?'

'It's my head. It really hurts.' Alice Baxter closed her eyes and pressed a hand to her cheek. 'I feel so hot and dizzy. I don't know what's the matter with me.'

'Probably a touch too much sun.' Sam smiled. 'But we'll check you over, just to be on the safe side. At least it's nice and cool in here.'

'I'm sorry to be such a bother.'

'You're not a bother at all. We just want you to be able to enjoy your day, so let's see what we can do to sort you out.'

Kate watched as Sam's fingers felt for the woman's pulse. He glanced up at her and she moved forward, smiling.

'Why don't I help you take off your cardigan, Mrs Baxter? I'm sure you'll be much cooler without it. And maybe your shoes?' She looked at the examination couch and at Sam.

He nodded. 'You might feel a bit better if you were to lie down for a while.'

Between them they helped Alice Baxter onto the couch where she lay with her eyes closed and a hand clasped to her head, while Alfred anxiously held her other hand.

Sam moved imperceptibly away and lowered his voice. 'I think it's heatstroke.'

'I agree. She's probably been wandering around in this heat without a hat for a couple of hours. It must be nearly eighty degrees out there.'

'Her pulse is racing and she obviously has a headache. I'm not surprised she's feeling ill.'

'She's certainly a bit confused. What is her temperature?'

'Over forty degrees. We need to get her cooled down. Ideally we could use a damp sheet.'

'I can probably find a sponge. We can bathe her with cool water. That should help to bring the temperature down and, hopefully, she'll start to feel better.'

'Let's get started straight away, then. The last thing we need is for her to lose consciousness.'

For the next half-hour they worked steadily, gently sponging and reassuring and checking the woman's progress. Within an hour Alice was sufficiently recovered to be able to get to her feet, assisted by her husband who was looking distinctly happier.

'You scared the living daylights out of me, woman.' He held her arm as they made their way out of the tent.

'Old fusspot.' She patted his hand.

'Well, there goes at least one happy customer.' Kate smiled. 'And now I suppose you'd like a cup of tea?'

'Sounds like a good idea to me.' Sam stretched and eased his aching muscles.

Kate looked at him and almost wished she hadn't. He was wearing jeans and a black T-shirt, which came untucked as he raised his arms above his head. She found herself gazing with fascination at the taut muscles of his stomach and felt the warm colour swim into her cheeks.

With jerky movements she began to gather up the equipment. 'You go.' Carefully avoiding his glance, she dropped the used linen into a bag and began checking her notes. 'I'll finish up here. We're not exactly rushed off our feet so you could take a half-hour break.'

He removed the pen from her grasp and drew her to her feet. 'We'll *both* go. You need a break as much as I do.'

'But—'

'Kate, a couple of the first-aiders can hold the fort for a while.'

She looked at him, all too conscious of his nearness.

His eyes glinted. 'I'm not a man to be argued with, Dr Dawson.'

No, Kate thought. She was beginning to realise that. Sam Slater was the kind of man who seemed to have a way of getting precisely what he wanted before you even knew what was happening. But right now she felt too hot and tired to argue.

'Let's go for a walk by the river. It'll be quieter and cooler down there.'

His hand was on her arm and he was leading her across the grass towards the edge of the field.

'Are you sure we won't be missed?'

'Does it matter?' He looked at her and smiled. 'We've had a busy morning. I think we're entitled to relax for a while, don't you?'

He was right. It certainly was cooler by the river. Sighing, Kate leaned against a tree, briefly closing her eyes as she listened to the sound of gently rippling water.

'Mmm. This is perfect. We should have brought a picnic.'

'Funny you should say that.' From his pocket Sam produced a bar of chocolate. 'Not quite the same, but it's the best I can do.' He broke the bar, proffering a piece. She took it and popped it into her mouth, relishing the milky sweetness as she sat on the grass.

Sam's mouth twitched slightly as he sat beside her. 'You have chocolate on your face. Here, let me.' He reached out a hand, gently removing the smudge from her cheek. 'You look about sixteen years old.'

But Kate didn't feel like a sixteen-year-old! Her head

jerked up and, almost as if he'd been expecting it, his mouth descended without warning over hers.

She moaned softly as her body responded traitorously. I'm so weak, she thought. Thoroughly spineless.

She gasped as his lips made a teasing but thorough foray over her eyes and cheek, nuzzling at her ear before returning to claim her mouth in a heated demand that banished the thought of resistance from her mind.

His hands moved to her hair, drawing her relentlessly closer, loosening the clips, and went on, remorselessly inviting responses which her body gave until she moaned softly.

This shouldn't be happening, she told herself. It was utterly crazy, but he seemed to have robbed her of the power to resist.

The spell was shattered as suddenly he stiffened, pulling away, and she uttered a soft moan of protest. What had she done wrong?

'Sam, what...?'

He rose to his feet and stared, grim-faced, past her to the field, crowded with families, enjoying the afternoon's events.

'There's a fire, Kate.' He was hauling her to her feet now. 'It looks as if one of the tents is ablaze. People could be hurt.'

She was already running, heading for the thin column of smoke which was drifting into the air, and the sound of cries of alarm drove her on.

'Where is it? I can't see...'

'It looks like the catering tent.' Sam was ahead of her. People were scattering in all directions as panic began to take hold, and she was forced briefly to a halt as the acrid smell of smoke caught in her throat.

'You stay here,' he said tersely.

'No chance, Sam. I'm coming with you.'

People were running from the tent. Tables were tipped over and crockery smashed in the ensuing panic.

'Is everyone out?' Sam's voice cracked with tension.

'Can't tell.' The steward shook his head. 'It all happened so quickly. The smoke's too thick to see.'

'Jason!' A woman screamed. 'My little boy's missing. He's only five.'

'When did you last see him?'

'Just a minute or two ago. I thought he was with me, then everyone started screaming and pushing. Oh, God, Jason, where are you?' Her voice broke.

Kate heard Sam's quick intake of breath.

'Go and ring the fire brigade,' she called to one of the men who was doing his best to usher everyone to safety.

'They're on the way. Luckily someone spotted the smoke. This way, folks. Stay calm. Just move away from the tent.'

Kate didn't stop to see if Sam was with her. Her only thought was that a child might be trapped, or lying unconscious. She held a hanky over her nose and mouth. Her eyes were already smarting from the insidious invasion of smoke.

Coughing, she began to feel her way across the tent with fingers that trembled.

'Kate, what the hell do you think you're doing? Get out of here, *now*!' Sam's voice came through the thickening smoke.

She ignored him. Somehow she had to find the child before the heat became too intense. 'We have to find him, Sam.' Her own voice was muffled by the hanky. She drew in a deep breath and coughed again as the smoke and heat were drawn into her lungs. 'He's only little. He won't survive long in this.'

'Kate, do as you're told. Get out *now*! The whole thing could go up in flames at any minute.'

'I'm not leaving until we find him, Sam.'

'Dammit, woman! You pick a fine time to argue.'

Sam made a grab for her and she pushed him away. His arms snaked round her waist and she struck out at him. She caught a brief glimpse of his grim expression, the strong lines of his face tough and uncompromising, before she was lifted, slung unceremoniously over his shoulder, and carried, protesting, as he headed for the fresh air.

'Here, hold onto her. Don't let her back in there.' Sam thrust her into the restraining arms of the steward, before turning and disappearing into the pall of thickening smoke.

Shakily, Kate twisted round and looked fearfully towards the tent. Her throat felt sore and her head was pounding. Minutes passed and there was still no sign of Sam. Suddenly, despite the heat, she was shivering violently.

'We have to do something,' she cried, her voice anguished, her eyes pleading. She tried to pull away but, frustratingly, the steward's grip tightened.

'I can't let you go in there, miss. There's nothing you can do.'

'But we can't let him do it alone.' The muscles of her stomach knotted in apprehension as she waited and watched for Sam to reappear. What if he was lying unconscious…?

It was only when, after what seemed like an eternity, he emerged, soot-blackened and coughing, carrying a small child in his arms, that Kate felt the gripping bands snap inside her.

'Sam.' Her heart contracted painfully as finally she broke free and ran towards him. She helped as shakily he handed the whimpering child over to his mother, to be ushered towards a waiting ambulance. Only then did Sam suddenly sag forward, his hands on his knees as he drew in several harsh, laboured breaths.

'You should go to hospital, Sam. You've inhaled a lot of smoke.'

He shook his head and straightened up, glancing back at the smoke-blackened tent, and they stood in silence as the licking flames began slowly to reduce it to a burnt-out shell.

Most of the crowd had dispersed to a safe distance, and now that the drama seemed to be over they began to drift away. 'You've scorched your arm.' Sam's voice was hoarse.

She glanced at the reddened mark and frowned. 'It's nothing. I'm fine.' Which was more than could be said for the rest of her, she thought. Her heart was thudding under her ribs and she was dismayed to feel the tears suddenly pricking at her eyelids. It was totally illogical. Shock, she told herself as she turned and made blindly for the car.

In two strides Sam caught and held her. 'Kate? What is it? What's wrong? Oh, God, you're not hurt?'

She swallowed hard, shaking her head. 'It's nothing. I told you. I'm fine.'

He ignored the denial, his breathing ragged as he held her, turning her roughly towards him. He tilted her face, frowning as she looked at him.

'Kate...? You're cross...'

She gave a slight laugh, her face taut with strain as she looked at him. 'Cross? Why should I be cross?' Something inside her snapped. He had risked his life and he wondered why she was angry? 'I suppose you do realise that what you did back there was totally irresponsible? Of all the pig-headed, arrogant—'.

She gasped as his hands tightened on her arms, told herself she would feel absolutely nothing as he pulled her body against the muscular hardness of his thighs before his mouth came down on hers.

What she hadn't counted on was the spontaneous response of every nerve in her body that simply being close to this man seemed to evoke.

She gasped as she felt a surge of pure physical awareness as the sensual mouth ground against hers.

She drew a ragged breath. He raised his glittering gaze to look at her and his mouth curved in gentle laugher.

'You have a smut on your nose.' He raised his hand to brush it away.

'I have news for you, Dr Slater,' she said breathlessly. 'You're not exactly looking your best either.' She leaned forward and sniffed hard. 'You smell of smoke.'

He threw back his head and laughed. 'Oh, Kate.' He looked at her and groaned softly. 'You must know how much I want you.' With a shuddering sigh he raised his head, muttering her name as his lips followed the line of her mouth and then her jaw, before returning to tease her mouth.

The sensation was electric. Kate hesitated for only a second, then her head went back as she let herself be swept along by a confusing vortex of emotions. She didn't want to fight the sense of urgency that was threatening to engulf her. It had been so long since her body had felt this kind of need, and with a sense of shock she realised that she was within a hair's breadth of falling in love with this man! If she wasn't very careful it could happen—if she chose to let it.

But what then? her inner voice warned. You've been down this path before and it didn't work. It could happen again.

A sob caught in her throat and she stiffened in his arms.

She tried to drag herself away and felt his arms tighten, saw the look of confusion in his eyes.

'Kate. what is it?'

'No, please, don't.' Kate closed her eyes, aware of the turmoil in Sam's eyes as she broke free, panicking as she realised how little it would take to make her surrender. If he kissed her again…

'I can't…I won't be hurt again. I've been through it and I don't intend to let it happen again. Don't you see? It's a risk I can't…I'm not prepared to take.'

Sam released her abruptly, his face taut as he stared grimly at her. 'You can't run away for ever, Kate. Someday it may just happen and you won't be able to fight it. You were unlucky. Yes, you were hurt, but you have to start trusting someone again, some time.'

She pressed a shaking hand to her mouth. 'I don't have to let it happen. I won't let it.' The words were whispered as he drew away, but she thought in sudden terror that it was already too late. She was already in love with Sam.

CHAPTER SEVEN

IT CAME as a relief in the week that followed not to have time even to think about Sam. It seemed as if summer had finally gone. Instead, the weather suddenly turned cold and with it came the almost inevitable spate of coughs and sore throats. And within days, as if to add to the chaos, an outbreak of chickenpox emptied the schools and filled the surgery.

Kate walked into Reception, smiling as she unfastened her jacket. 'Morning, folks.'

'Good morning. You're nice and early. What's the matter? Couldn't sleep or something?'

Kate smiled ruefully. 'I was called out at five this morning. By the time I got back it was hardly worth going back to bed.'

'Oh, poor you.'

'I'll survive—just. With another cup of very strong, black coffee.'

'Coming up.' Smiling, Lucy handed Kate the mail and Kate flicked through it, resigned to the inevitable pharmaceutical promotions advising her of the very latest in drugs and medical care.

'All the usual gripping stuff, I see. Is that one for me?'
'Afraid so.'

She peered at the list of calls and messages. 'It looks as if it's going to be another busy morning.'

'Oh, Doctor.' Lucy glanced up as Sam walked into Reception. 'I've just got the results of that blood test you were waiting for. It came in this morning's mail. I know it's here somewhere. Ah, yes.' Rummaging among the papers on the desk, she handed over a sheet of paper.

Sam glanced at it briefly. 'Well, thank goodness for that. It's clear. At least now I can put Charlie Forbes's mind at rest and he can get on with his life.'

He straightened up, his eyes locking briefly with Kate's. A spasm flickered briefly across his face before he nodded and strode away.

He looked tired, too, she thought. She drew a shaky breath and pushed a hand through her hair. On the point of following him, she felt something hold her back. After all, what was there to say? He'd said she had to start trusting someone some time and she did trust him. But even Sam couldn't predict what the future might hold. So many things could change. *People* could change.

The only thing she was certain of was that she felt the distance between them as painfully as if it were tangible. But at least there was safety in distance.

'I suppose I'd better make a start.' She gave a slight smile. 'I don't suppose you could manage to find a couple of aspirin to go with that coffee?'

'Will do, and I'll give you a couple of minutes before I send in the first patient.'

'You're an angel.'

In her own room, Kate dropped the bundle of files on to her desk and drew a deep breath, before shedding her coat and going to check her appearance in the mirror—neatly tailored brown trousers, high-necked, tan-coloured sweater.

Seating herself at the desk, she drained her cup of coffee when it arrived, swallowed the aspirin and pressed the buzzer to summon her first patient.

'Mrs Lucas.' Kate looked up, smiling as the woman came hesitantly into the consulting room. 'Come in. Sit down and tell me what I can do for you.'

May Lucas, according to her notes, was sixty-four. Her face was pale, she was thin and she moved awkwardly to sit in the chair.

'I'm not sure what you can do, Doctor. I feel a bit of a fraud, wasting your time like this…'

'You're not wasting my time at all,' Kate smiled reassuringly. 'I'm here to help if I can. Something is obviously troubling you. Why not try to tell me about it?'

The woman shivered, hugging her coat round her as she seemed to struggle to concentrate. 'It's just that I'm always so cold, even on a warm day.' Her speech was slow and hesitant. 'I feel such a fool when other folk are out in their summer clothes and I'm wearing a sweater.'

Kate glanced, frowning, at the computer screen. 'I gather you've seen Dr Parker several times during the past nine months or so.'

'Yes, that's right. I'd been getting a lot of pain in my joints—here.' She gently kneaded the swollen, arthritic fingers of her right hand. 'It's a real nuisance, I don't mind telling you. I used to do a bit of knitting but I can't any more.'

Kate moved to gently examine the woman's hands and wrists, noting the redness of the inflamed joints. May winced slightly and Kate frowned.

'Is it just your hands, or are any other joints affected?'

'My knees and my feet.'

Nodding, Kate returned to sit at her desk where she re-read the notes, recognising the name of a well-known anti-inflammatory drug which she knew to be extremely beneficial in cases such as May Lucas's.

'I see you had the last course of painkillers about three months ago. Do you find they help?'

'Not really, to be honest.'

'Let me just check your pulse.' Kate reached for the

woman's wrist, noting as she did so that May Lucas seemed short of breath. Somewhere in Kate's head, tiny alarm bells were beginning to ring. Something about what should have been a straightforward case of rheumatoid arthritis didn't seem to be running quite true to form.

Kate frowned. May's pulse was racing and she was shivering violently, despite the fact that the consulting room was warm. She sat back. 'It's not very warm today, is it, Mrs Lucas?'

May glanced uncertainly at the window where drops of rain drifted against the glass. 'No, I suppose it's not.'

Kate smiled. 'I prefer the summer myself. I like to be warm, don't you?'

'I don't think it makes much difference. Summer or winter, I never feel warm.'

'Have you lost weight recently, May?'

The woman nodded, her face anxious. 'I had to buy another skirt the other day. The others seem to be looser than they were. Why, Doctor? You don't...you don't think anything's wrong, do you?'

'I'd just like to check something, May.' Kate rose to her feet. 'Do you ever have pain in your jaw or ears?'

The woman nodded. 'Well, yes. But I didn't think too much of it. I mean, you do get funny little aches and pains as you get older, don't you?'

'Yes, I'm afraid that's true.' Kate smiled. 'I'd like to take a look at your neck, May. I'll try not to hurt you.'

She made a gentle but thorough examination of the woman's neck, concentrating on the area next to the windpipe, then returned to her seat.

'Look, I'd like to try you on some different tablets, May. I think you'll find them more effective than the ones you've been taking.'

The woman's eyes widened. 'Different? But why?'

Kate smiled. 'Have you noticed that you haven't been feeling too well lately? You said you always feel cold. Have you noticed that you've been a little forgetful, too?'

May laughed slightly, but Kate was quick to notice that her eyes had filled with tears. 'I thought perhaps I was going a bit daft in my old age.'

Kate gently placed her hand over the woman's fingers. 'I can promise you, you're not going daft, May.'

'But what's wrong with me, then?'

Kate frowned. 'I'll need to do a blood test.' She saw the look of anxiety on the woman's face. 'It's really nothing to worry about. It's just that all your symptoms seem to point to a thyroid deficiency, but I can't confirm it, or treat you accordingly, until it's confirmed.'

'Thyroid? No! Well, I never. My mother had problems with her thyroid, too.'

'Well, there we are, then.' Kate smiled. 'These things often run in families.'

'So what happens now?'

'I'll just need a blood sample. If you see Sue, our nurse, before you leave, she'll see to that for you. It only takes a few seconds and it won't hurt at all. We'll send that off to the hospital.'

'And how long will it be before we get the results?'

Kate reached for her notepad. 'It shouldn't be too long. What I'd like you to do is make an appointment to see me again next week. Hopefully the test results will be through by then and we can take things from there. We can start you on a course of replacement therapy.'

'And is that it? Will I feel better? It all sounds too good to be true.'

'Ah, well, not quite. I'll need to see you at regular intervals, just to be sure that the medication is doing what it's supposed to do and that it suits you. We need to start you on a tiny dose and build it up slowly. But, apart from that, yes, hopefully, you'll soon be feeling much better.'

She rose to her feet to see the woman out, and May left, smiling. Kate returned to her desk and pressed the buzzer for her next patient, who turned out to be a runny-nosed seven-year-old who slumped into a chair and swung his legs, kicking the desk, watched by his weary-faced mother.

Kate glanced at her notes. 'It's young Paul, isn't it?' She smiled at the boy.

'It's his chest, Doctor. His cough's not getting any better and he's had it for near on a month.' The woman sighed. 'I don't know what to do with him.'

Kate reached for her stethoscope. 'Why don't I just have a listen to your chest, Paul? See if we can see what's going on in there.'

The boy looked at her and wiped the back of his hand across his nose but made no other attempt to move.

'Paul! Let the doctor listen to your chest.'

'I promise I won't hurt you.' Kate smiled. 'I don't suppose you enjoy feeling poorly. Perhaps we can do something to make you feel better.'

Reluctantly he got to his feet, sighing heavily. His mother began tugging at his shirt. 'I'll be glad when he's back at school.'

Kate smiled. 'Do you like school, Paul?'

'He won't like it when he gets back and has to catch up on all the work he's missed. Paul, behave! Let the doctor listen to your chest.'

Kate felt her hackles rise. Gently she applied the stethoscope, listening carefully, and frowned. 'Right, you can tuck your shirt in again, Paul. I'll just quickly check your ears.' Reaching for the auroscope, she showed it to the child. 'I just want to shine this light into your ears so that I can see if there's any redness or infection.'

'You keep still now, Paul. Let the doctor have a look in your ears.'

Kate stifled a sigh. Seated at the desk again, she said, 'Right, well they seem to be clear.' Studying the notes on the computer, she frowned. 'Paul's ears are clear but he does still seem to have a bit of a chest infection. I see from his notes that Dr Blake saw Paul about a month ago and prescribed a course of antibiotics. When did he actually finish the course?'

Ann Miller fumbled in her handbag. 'I can't remember exactly. it's not easy, you know? Paul's not the only one. I can't always keep track...'

'He *did* finish the course, Mrs Miller?'

'Well, he may have done. I'm not sure. He seemed so much better, there didn't seem much point.'

Kate sat back in her chair. 'Mrs Miller, it's always important to finish a course of antibiotics, even though Paul may have been feeling better, otherwise what can sometimes happen is that the infection doesn't clear properly and sometimes it comes back, only worse, a second time.'

She typed out a new prescription. 'I'm going to give you another prescription. We'll try something slightly different, but this time you must make sure Paul finishes the course. There we are.' She tore it off and handed it to the woman. 'That should do the trick.' She ruffled the child's hair. 'If you're at all worried come and see me again.'

When the last patient had finally left, Kate made her way to the small staffroom to find Tim making coffee.

'Ah, just the person I wanted to see.'

'That sounds ominous.'

He grinned. 'Coffee?'

'Just a gallon.'

'That bad?'

Smiling, she took the cup he handed to her and helped

herself to sugar. 'No, not really. Sometimes I just wonder why we're here. I mean, the patient sits there, tells you her troubles. You provide what you hope will be a cure and then they decide they know best after all.'

Tim laughed. 'I know what you mean.' He helped himself to a biscuit. 'I've had a few of those myself. I decided it goes with the territory. No point letting it get you down.'

'I'll try to remember that. Mmm, this coffee is good.' She frowned. 'Did you say you wanted to see me?'

'It's nothing desperately important. There are a few things I thought I should hand over, things I don't want to leave unfinished while I'm away.'

'It's all right for some.' Sue and Lucy walked into the staffroom. Lucy sank into a chair, kicked off her shoes and kneaded her toes. 'Oh, that feels good.' Her mouth quirked. 'Where exactly did you say you were going on this honeymoon of yours?'

Tim looked at her with amused eyes. 'I didn't. It's a secret. Nice try, though.'

'Spoilsport.'

He grinned and handed a folder to Kate. 'I don't think there's anything desperately urgent. Obviously I'll still be dealing with things, day to day, while I'm here, but I thought you might want to have a glance through these. I'm waiting for the results of a blood test on Mrs Harriman.'

'What's the problem?' Kate flipped one of the pages.

'I suspect it might be glandular fever. I suggested she ring for the results towards the end of next week.'

'Fine. I'll have a chat with her. What's this?'

Tim glanced over her shoulder. 'Patrick Peters. Oh, yes, his arthritis has been getting steadily worse. His knees have just about packed up altogether. I've had a word with the surgeon chappie on the mainland, and he's going to try to bring Patrick's operation forward. It's possible he may get back to me before I go away, but, just in case...'

'Do you want me to go and see him?'

'If you can fit it in—unless I've managed to visit him myself before then.'

'No problem. I have to go out that way some time, anyway, to see Ed Bristow. I can kill two birds with one stone. Anything else?'

'Just a few notes. Everything is in the folder.' He drained his coffee and put the cup down. Glancing at his watch, he headed for the door. 'Well, this won't do. Can't sit here all day. Some of us have work to do.'

He was gone, grinning as a magazine flew through the air, missing him by inches as the door closed.

Kate looked at her own watch. 'He's right. I shouldn't be here either. By the way, I don't suppose you know where last month's copy of the *Medical Journal* is, do you? There was a write-up on a new drug I particularly wanted to read. I think it may be relevant to a case I'm dealing with.'

She hunted, frowning, through a pile of journals on the table. 'All the rest seem to be here.'

'I think Sam may have it. He mentioned the particular article I think you mean a couple of days ago.' Lucy got to her feet to glance at a stack of journals on the shelf. 'No, it's not here.'

'Damn!' Kate muttered under her breath. Draining her cup, she put it down. 'I'll see if he's still in his room. See you later.'

She walked along the corridor, coming to a halt outside Sam's door. Her heart thudded as her hand rose to knock. Did she really want the journal so badly? Yes, she did, damn it. She had recently diagnosed a patient with Alzheimer's disease, and had been particularly interested to read of a possible new treatment. Her hand hung, poised in mid-air. This was ridiculous. Sooner or later she had to face him.

Kate tapped lightly on the door and, for a moment, no one answered. He was out. Oh, well, the evil hour could be postponed. With a feeling of relief she'd turned away when the door opened and he was standing there, a look of surprise on his face, while she stood rooted to the spot.

Sam frowned. 'Did you want to see me?'

She swallowed hard. 'No, it's not... Well, yes, as a matter of fact.'

His dark brows drew together. 'I was just about to start my visits. Is it urgent?'

'No, probably not, or at least...' She summoned a smile. 'I was rather hoping to read an article on Alzheimer's in last month's journal. Lucy thought you might have it, but it doesn't matter. It can wait.'

He paused, then stepped back into the room. 'You'd better come in. It's here somewhere.' Frowning, he moved a pile of papers on his desk and glanced at the bookshelf. 'I'm sure I had it here.'

'Look, it really doesn't matter.'

'It may be in the car. Perhaps I can let you have it later?'

'Sure. That's fine.'

He looked at her, his expression unreadable, and for some reason she felt cheated. How could he behave as if nothing had happened? But, then, she told herself, nothing had.

'Yes, well, I'd better let you get on.'

'How are things?'

'Oh—fine.'

'Any news of Doug?'

She turned to the taut face watching her. 'I spoke to Elizabeth a few days ago. She says they're just waiting for the call from the hospital to say they're going ahead with

Doug's operation. She says he seems to be bearing up remarkably well, but it must be a difficult time for both of them.'

'I'm sure it is.' Sam's eyes were dark and unsmiling as he turned, frowning impatiently as he reached for his mobile phone. He dropped it into his briefcase and snapped the locks. 'Anyway, I'd better make a start on these calls.'

It was like talking to a stranger, except that the face was the same, perhaps a little more weary, and suddenly she found herself battling against an urge to rush into his arms.

She drew a ragged breath. 'Sam, we need to talk.' She half turned to follow him, almost colliding with Jill, who was hovering apologetically in the corridor.

'Oh, Dr Slater, I'm sorry to interrupt, but there's a phone call for you. It sounds rather urgent.'

He looked at his watch, his dark brows drawing together. 'Damn! I'm just on my way out. I'm already late. Can you take a message?'

'I think it's a personal call, Doctor. From the mainland. A Dr Dupres? She did say it was urgent that she speak to you.'

'Marie-Laure?' He frowned. 'You're sure she was calling from this country?'

'She made a point of saying the mainland.'

'I'll take it in my office.' Glancing at Kate, he said, 'Look, I'm sorry, was it something important? Perhaps we can catch up with each other later?'

'No.' With an effort Kate managed to smile and felt her heart contract with misery as she watched him stride away. 'No, it wasn't important at all.'

The cottage didn't seem to offer the usual comfort when she returned to it later that evening, possibly because the debris from several cups of coffee still littered the kitchen and the fire had gone out.

Sighing, she abandoned her jacket, flipped the switch on the kettle and hurried upstairs to change into a comfortable pair of jeans and a sweater.

Her reflection stared back at her, ridiculously childlike, but there was nothing she could do about that, she decided. She made her way to the kitchen to make coffee and reheat a casserole she had prepared the night before, only to find that her appetite had completely vanished.

Her thoughts were in turmoil as she sat at the kitchen table, sipping at a cup of scalding hot coffee. She felt confused and unsettled, dazed by her reaction to a man she scarcely knew, incapable of understanding fully the tumult of sensations she had experienced in Sam's arms. Pleasure, confusion, excitement—all the things she'd promised herself she would never feel again.

The truth was that, since the disastrous break-up of her marriage to Colin, she had kept her emotions in cold storage, telling herself that that way they were safe. What she hadn't bargained for was that someone might come along, someone like Sam, and rekindle the fires. And now, suddenly, all of her carefully built barriers were in grave danger of being toppled.

Sighing, she got to her feet and tipped the dregs of coffee into the sink. She hadn't really wanted it anyway. Her heart didn't need the added boost of caffeine, it was unsteady enough without it!

She removed the hot casserole from the oven, wincing as she juggled it onto the top of the cooker, burning her hand in the process, and was sucking her finger when the doorbell rang.

'Damn!' She hurried to answer it and, as if her thoughts had somehow managed to conjure him up, Sam stood there.

He was wearing jeans and a dark blue sweatshirt that seemed to emphasise the colour of his eyes. He was holding a journal.

'I found that article you were interested in. I thought you might like to have it.'

'It could have waited.' She blew on her throbbing fingers and shook them. 'Look, you'd better come in. I was just taking something out of the oven.'

'That looks like a nasty burn.' Sam frowned, following her as she sped to the kitchen to switch off the rice she had put on to boil. 'You'd better let me take a look. Burns can be devilishly painful things.'

'It's nothing.' Her breath caught in her throat as his strong hand closed firmly over her wrist, sending absurd, tingling sensations travelling down her spine.

Against her better judgement she forced herself to relax, sensing that in any kind of battle with this man, she would be the loser.

'You see?' She averted her gaze from the stinging, red blister. 'It's a simple burn.'

'Even a simple burn can be painful.' He studied the reddening weal and frowned. 'Here…' he turned on the cold-water tap '…hold it under here until it cools down a bit.'

He held her hand as if she were a child, but there was nothing even remotely childlike in the way her body was responding to his nearness.

That was the trouble—common sense seemed to fly out of the window whenever Sam was around.

'I'll put a dressing on it for you.'

'I can do that,' Kate muttered through clenched teeth.

'Are you always this stubborn?'

Only when her self-control was in danger of snapping, she thought. Above her his face was shadowed, his expression unreadable.

Then, ignoring her protests, he went out to his car and came back with some cooling salve, which he applied to her arm.

'How's that?' he asked.

'Much easier. Thanks.'

She saw him frown, then a muscle pulsed rigidly in his jaw, the sensual mouth so tormentingly close to hers that her face tilted to meet it, drawing in the warm male scent of him.

The pain of her hand was forgotten. How could she ever have imagined that she could remain immune?

She moaned softly as his mouth came slowly down on hers, making gentle advances against her cheek, to the hollow of her throat and back to her lips, and before she knew it she was caught within the circle of his arms.

'Kate,' he said huskily. He cupped her face in his hands. his lips brushed against her mouth, sending exquisite shivers racing down her spine. 'Have you any idea what being close to you does to me?'

How could she not know? She moaned softly as his mouth covered hers, moving with frustrating sensuality.

'Sam, this is crazy,' she protested weakly. 'I thought we'd agreed—'

'I don't remember agreeing to anything,' he said softly. 'Ask me to stay, Kate.'

'This isn't fair.' Her body quivered beneath the onslaught. She moaned as his hands slid beneath her sweater, discovering the rounded firmness of her breasts. It was utterly crazy, she told herself.

'Sam, this isn't a good idea,' she protested weakly. Her eyes closed, she tilted her head back, trying to give herself time to think. Nothing had changed. The risks were still there, always would be there. What she had with Sam now was wonderful, but what about when it all turned sour? And it would, because it always did.

'Tell me you want me to stay, Kate,' he breathed again, before his teeth nibbled at the very sensitive lobe of her ear.

She heard her own soft gasp of shock as the contact renewed all the fire of their previous encounters. 'I—I can't,' she groaned softly. 'You know why I can't. It won't work, Sam. Please, don't ask me.'

'Don't fight it, Kate. You know you don't want to. Go with it,' he rasped. 'There's nothing to be afraid of.'

But there was. There was everything to be afraid of. History had a habit of repeating itself. Her parents... Colin...

'Things like this don't happen.'

'They do if you let them. You've got to want it, Kate.'

'I'm scared. You don't understand. It's not that simple.'

'But it can be.' His shuddering breath whispered against the pale perfection of her skin. 'You have to let go of the past, Kate. That's all it takes. Believe in the future, believe in us.'

He made it sound so easy, and maybe it was. Maybe he was right. If you wanted something badly enough it was possible to make it work. She had made a mistake in trusting Colin—a bad mistake, and she had paid the price. But this time it could be different—couldn't it? Such a small step to take.

Sam bent his head to kiss her again and she was incapable of thinking of anything except the warm pressure of his mouth against hers. She responded unashamedly, moving restlessly, searching for some kind of fulfilment that seemed only just out of reach, almost drowning in sensations unlike any she had ever experienced before.

'Don't fight it, Kate. Don't think, don't try to understand. Just let it happen.'

It was mad, but she would think about that later, much later. Right now, all she could think of, *wanted* to think of, was that it seemed right.

Her senses felt drugged. She wasn't even aware of her fingers having made contact with the warm, silky smoothness of his skin beneath his shirt…

It was the sound of the phone ringing that brought her back to reality. Sam swore softly under his breath as, instinctively, she tried to move away.

'Ignore it.' His lips drew her back, but with the strident ringing, common sense returned rapidly and she pushed him gently away, trying to steady her breathing.

'You know I can't. It might be a patient. I have to answer it, Sam.'

She heard him curse under his breath as she reached behind her for the phone, fumbling for the receiver as Sam's marauding mouth followed her own until she tilted her head out of reach and said breathlessly, 'Dr Dawson. Yes. Yes, of course you were right to phone me.'

Sam nibbled wickedly at her ear. In desperation she pushed away as the voice said, 'Kate, I'm really sorry to call you at home.'

Kate straightened up, the laughter slipping from her eyes. 'Paula? What's the problem?'

'It's young William. I'm really worried about him. he's had this tummyache for a while and it seems to be getting worse. Can you come?'

'Yes, of course I will, straight away. Try not to worry.'

She was aware of Sam straightening up, his face suddenly expressionless. She wanted desperately to draw him back, to regain the moment, but it was already too late. Her eyes followed him to the door, silently pleading with him to wait.

'I'm really sorry, Kate,' the woman's voice repeated anxiously in her ear.

'Paula, don't be. It's always best to play safe, especially when a child complains of pain. I'll be about…twenty minutes.'

What she wanted to say was, I need some time for myself right now. But she dropped the receiver back into place and turned to look at the door, his face suddenly like that of a stranger again. The kiss might never have been, except that her lips still felt swollen from the pressure of his mouth.

'I have to go, Sam.'

'Of course you do,' he said evenly. 'It's all right, Kate. I understand. You don't have to explain.'

But as the door closed behind him she was shocked to find her eyes filling with tears.

'Damn!' She swore under her breath. 'Damn! Damn! Damn!'

Paula Davies was waiting for her at her front door as Kate brought the car to a halt.

She was in her late twenties, petite and blonde-haired, and her face was anxious as she ushered Kate into the house.

'Kate, I'm really sorry to have to call you out. I thought about bringing William to the surgery this morning, but he was sleeping and I thought…well, I was hoping he might be feeling better by now.'

'Obviously he isn't.'

'No. He's through here.'

Kate followed her.

'We thought it might be easier to keep an eye on him if he snuggled down on the sofa.' She led the way into the sitting room where a young man rose to his feet, a look of relief on his face as Kate walked into the room.

'Mike, how are you? I haven't seen you for a while.'

'I'm fine.' He pulled a wry face. 'I've been doing a lot of overtime just lately—the company's expanding. You know what it's like.' He gave her a slight grin. 'It's this young man who's the problem.'

'Hello, William.' Kate bent to brush a finger gently against the six-year-old's cheek. He was lying on the sofa. His eyes were closed and his knees were drawn up beneath the blanket.

Brushing a hand gently against his forehead, Kate could feel that he had a temperature. 'Mummy says you're not feeling too well. Can you tell me where it hurts?'

A small hand came out from beneath the blanket and settled in the area of his lower abdomen.

'When precisely did it start?' She turned to look at her friend.

'This morning. He complained of having a tummyache. We thought maybe he was a bit constipated. We thought it was something he'd eaten, only he seemed to get worse.'

The couple watched anxiously as Kate made a gentle but thorough examination, before finally straightening up.

'Did he complain that the pain started in a particular place?'

'Well, yes, to the right, but it moved.'

Kate nodded, watching every fleeting change of expression on the child's face. 'And where is the pain now, William? Here? Yes, that's all right, sweetheart. I've finished now.' She gave swift, smiling reassurance and tucked the blanket round the small figure again. 'Has he been sick?'

'Yes, twice.'

Kate nodded. 'And he has a temperature.'

'Do you know what's wrong with him, Kate?'

'Well, I can tell you it's nothing desperately serious.' She lowered her voice as they moved away from the bed. 'All the same, I'm afraid I'm going to have to get him admitted to hospital. It's appendicitis. He's obviously in a lot of pain, so the sooner we get him admitted the better.'

'I had a feeling that's what you were going to say.' Even so, Paula looked concerned. 'I had it myself when I was a kid. Mind you, I was nearly twelve.'

Kate smiled as she reached for her mobile phone. 'Yes, well, you'll probably remember what it was like, and that the only thing you wanted was for someone to take the pain away. So I'll ring through for an ambulance now, and we'll probably have him settled in at the hospital within the hour.'

'I suppose I'd better go and get a few things together in an overnight bag?' In spite of her obvious relief, Paula was a little tearful. 'He won't want to go without his teddy. Will they operate tonight?'

'Probably.' Kate put an arm round the woman's shoulders. 'I know you're worried,' she said softly, 'but, I promise you, he's going to be feeling a lot better once they get rid of what's causing the pain.'

'I don't know how to thank you...'

'Hey, there's no need. It's what I'm here for.'

Mike smiled. 'This job must play havoc with your social life.'

And then some, Kate thought. Twenty minutes later she was on her way back to the cottage. It was late. She felt physically tired, emotionally exhausted, and yet, frustratingly, she knew that even if she went to bed she wouldn't sleep. Mentally her brain was in turmoil.

The lights were still on in Sam's cottage as she drove through the village. Almost involuntarily she brought the car to a halt. She switched off the engine but made no attempt to move, staring out into the darkness instead.

Her hands clenched the wheel. Suddenly she knew she couldn't leave things as they were. It was too untidy. Too much had been left unsaid, unfinished. The more she thought about it, the more she realised that, whether she liked it or not, Sam had become an important factor in her life.

The truth was that she had kept her emotions in cold storage for so long, imagining they were safe. What she hadn't expected had been someone like Sam coming along and rekindling the fire, and the trouble with fires, as she had learned the hard way, was that you could get more than your fingers burned.

She closed her eyes briefly, resting her head back. She had trusted Colin and he had betrayed her—more than once—as she had discovered in the two years their marriage had lasted. And now Sam was asking her to take a leap in the dark. Well, maybe he was right. If she was ever going to get on with her life, she had to start trusting again. For the first time in a long while, she felt she was doing something with her eyes wide open.

Taking a deep breath, she got out of the car. Standing outside Sam's cottage, she raised her hand, hesitated for a second, then knocked.

The sound of music from a stereo faded and a few seconds later the door opened. Then Sam was standing there, solid, dependable and very, very desirable. He didn't invite her in.

She swallowed hard and with an effort managed a smile. 'I'm sorry, I've only just realised how late it is, but I've been thinking... You were right, Sam, we do need to talk. So why don't you come over to my place for a meal? Tomorrow night? Or at the weekend, if that suits you better? Nothing fancy. I know you like pasta. We could open a bottle of wine and…'

Panic gave an edge to her voice. She looked at him, moistening her dry lips with her tongue. He wasn't making this easy. 'Or if Saturday isn't convenient…'

'As a matter of fact, no, it isn't.' His voice sounded rough-edged with tension. 'I'm sorry.'

'No. I see,' Kate said flatly, feeling the colour darken her cheeks as she looked at him. With an effort she managed to force a smile. 'Oh, well, not to worry. It was just an idea. Some other time maybe.' She had half turned away when his voice stopped her.

'Kate, wait.'

'It's all right.' She gave a slight laugh. 'You don't need to explain.' She was fumbling with the car door handle when his voice stopped her.

'It's not that I don't appreciate the offer. It's just that I'm afraid I won't be here. I need to go away for a few days. I'm sorry if it's going to cause some inconvenience, but I was rather hoping you'd cover for me tomorrow.'

She was conscious of a sudden feeling of tightness in her throat. 'I see.' She took a deep breath and managed a smile. 'Yes, of course.'

'It is important.'

'Yes, I'm sure it must be.'

A spasm flickered briefly across Sam's features. 'Something cropped up unexpectedly. There are a few things I need to discuss with Marie-Laure.'

Marie-Laure. The call from the mainland. Kate's throat tightened painfully. Of course, she hadn't made the connection until now. Suddenly it all made sense. Shock seemed to hold her rooted to the spot, even though her instinct was to turn and walk away. Marie Laure, the girl from his past...except that it seemed she was suddenly very much a part of the present.

She swallowed hard. 'I thought she was in Africa.'

'So did I.' Sam's mouth curved in a wry response. 'It seems she's over here for a visit and to attend a conference on world aid.'

Kate was shocked to discover that she could actually feel jealous of a girl she had never even met. How could she have been so naïve?

Sam's gaze narrowed. 'I thought, as you were on call anyway...'

'I'm sure I can cope.' She heard the note of irritation in her voice, but was powerless to stop it. She took a deep breath and even managed to smile. 'I'll manage.'

'I really am grateful.' He looked tired. Lines of strain and tension were etched around his mouth and eyes.

'I'll say goodnight, then.' Without waiting to hear his reply, she turned and hurried away.

CHAPTER EIGHT

IT WAS raining heavily when Kate drove to the surgery a couple of days later. Easing the car carefully along the narrow lanes, she braked to avoid a pool of water lying across the road.

She'd slept badly and, consequently, when she finally had drifted off she'd slept so heavily that she'd failed to hear the alarm.

That's all I need, she thought, grabbing a hastily made cup of coffee before dashing out to the car. Her head ached and the sight of a full waiting room did nothing to ease her temper.

Pausing at the desk to pick up the morning's list and patients' cards, she flicked through the morning's post and frowned.

'Damn! I was expecting the results of Mrs Peters's X-ray. I was sure it would be here today.'

'It's possible it might come in the second delivery.' Jill glanced at the clock. 'Postie is usually here again by mid-morning. Was it urgent?'

'Yes, it was. I need to know whether I can start her on a course of antibiotics or to refer her on to the specialist. Why the heck can't these people get their act together?'

Lucy looked over Kate's shoulder. 'I can phone through to the X-ray department for you, if it will help.'

'Yes... No.' Kate racked a hand through her hair, missing the look that passed between the two women. 'When is Mrs Peters due to see me again?'

Jill flipped through the pages of the appointments diary. 'Beginning of next week.'

'Oh, well, in that case I suppose it can wait another twenty-four hours, but if it's not here tomorrow...'

'Don't worry. I'll start chasing them.' Jill's smile became a look of concern as she followed Kate along the corridor. 'Do you feel all right? You're looking a bit peaky.'

'I've got a bit of a headache, that's all. Must be the weather or something.'

Jill smiled. 'Yes, I expect that's it. Oh, one good bit of news. I spoke to Mrs Matthews yesterday evening.'

'Mathews.' Kate frowned. 'Oh, yes. What's happened?'

'Well, it seems they've managed to locate Ed Bristow's missing daughter. You know there was a bit of a family tiff a few years ago and the family haven't spoken to each other since?'

'I heard the daughter had moved away from the area.'

'Yes, that's right. Well, it seemed no one had the daughter's new address—or at least they *thought* no one had it, but it seems someone local had kept in touch. Just the occasional Christmas card. You know how it is. Anyway, it seems she heard that Ted hadn't been too well, so she wrote to the daughter and Mrs Matthews got a phone call. They're all going to get together. So it looks like things could work out after all.'

'Oh, I'm glad.' At least some people got a happy ending. Kate thought about Sam. 'Were there any other messages?'

Jill shook her head and smiled. 'No. It must be your lucky day.'

No news of when Sam expected to be back, then. She hadn't realised quite how desperately she would miss hearing his voice, how much she wanted to talk to him, and she was unprepared for the intense surge of disappointment that swept over her.

Then common sense took over. What was there to say? He was busy getting reacquainted with Marie-Laure, the woman who had made him feel that life was still worth living. Kate felt her throat tighten painfully.

Better put her mind to other things. She sighed as the door opened, letting in a waft of cold, damp air, and a harassed-looking mum with a three-year-old and a baby came into Reception.

'I just need to make a phone call then I'll get started.'

'I'll pop these cards into Sue's treatment room, then I'll make you a cup of coffee. You look as if you need it.'

'You're a lifesaver.' Kate gave a grin of apology.

Why was it, she wondered, as she pressed the buzzer an hour later, that when she was having a bad day anyway, things which would normally have been straightforward turned into something of a nightmare?

Jim Fothergill was an overweight, ruddy-complexioned sixty-year-old who knew his rights and wasn't about to be denied them. He leaned forward, his fingers rapping the desk.

'I always saw the other doctor. Dr Parker.'

'Yes, Mr Fothergill. Unfortunately, Dr Parker has left the practice—'

'Not exactly considerate of him, was it? Patients don't seem to count for nothing these days. Service gets worse and worse.'

Kate stifled a sigh. 'I hope that's not true, Mr Fothergill. We do try to do our best. Perhaps if you tell me what the problem is, I may be able to help.'

'It's my foot, isn't it?' He thrust out one leg. 'Damn thing.'

'You do look rather uncomfortable.'

'Uncomfortable! I've been in agony.'

'If you slip off your shoe and sock, I can take a look. How long has it been bothering you?'

'It's been nigh on a week now.'

'Yes, I see.' Kate made a careful examination of the swollen foot. 'It must be painful to walk on it.'

'Well, of course it is. Damn thing swollen up like a balloon. How could it not be painful?' He grunted as she gently pressed the side of his big toe. 'I couldn't hardly get my shoe on this morning.'

'Yes, I can see. It feels hot, too. OK, Mr Fothergill, you can pop your shoe back on now.' Straightening up, Kate entered a few details into the computer, before looking at him. 'Well, what you've got, I'm afraid, is gout.'

'Gout!' Jim Fothergill was horrified. 'No. You're wrong. Are you saying I'm a drinker? Nay, I don't drink more than a glass of beer a week, and I never touch—'

'Mr Fothergill.' Kate smiled reassuringly. 'I promise you, gout has nothing to do with the amount of alcohol you drink. That's an old wives' tale. Anyone can get gout. It's caused by a build-up of uric acid crystals in the joint.'

Jim looked relieved. 'Thank God for that. I don't want folk around here thinking I'm a secret tippler.' He frowned. 'This isn't going to mean a visit to hospital, is it? I can't abide hospitals.'

'No, Mr Fothergill, no hospital.' Kate smiled. 'I'll give you prescription for some tablets. I'm sure you'll find they'll sort the problem out in no time.'

She watched him hobble out of the consulting room, not a happy man but appeased, and Kate turned to her next patient.

Half an hour later she walked through to Reception, depositing the bundle of record cards and a folder of letters on the desk in front of Lucy.

'Sorry about this. There are a couple of letters I need to go off tonight.'

'No problem. Things have quietened down a bit so I'll do them now and get them into the last post for you.'

'You're an angel.'

Tim walked into Reception. He eased his aching shoulders and stifled a jaw-cracking yawn. 'Lord, it's been a long morning. I could do with a coffee. How about you?'

Kate looked at her watch and ruefully shook her head. 'Nice idea but I'd better not. I've still got a few visits to do.'

'You look tired.'

'I am. The day seemed to start off badly and went rapidly down hill. Jim Fothergill came in.'

'Ah. Say no more.'

Tim dropped his mobile phone into his pocket and picked up his briefcase. 'I gather Sam's had to go away for a few days?'

'Yes. I forgot it was your day off yesterday so you wouldn't know.'

'Urgent, was it?'

'So I gather,' she said briskly. 'I could do with a couple of days off myself.'

'I know the feeling.'

She grinned. 'Well, it's all right for some. At least you and Theresa will be getting on that plane and heading for…wherever it is in, what…twenty-four hours from now?'

'I know, and I can hardly wait.' More seriously, he said, 'I'm sure Sam wouldn't have gone unless it was important.' He looked at her for a moment. 'Are you coping? I gather he asked you to cover for him?'

'Yes, of course. I'm fine.' She gave him a smile. But it wasn't entirely true, she reflected later as she drove home.

The truth, was she missed Sam. And, worse than that, she'd discovered that she was jealous.

It made no sense, she knew that. She didn't even know Marie-Laure Dupres. But that didn't prevent her wondering just how much this girl meant to Sam if she only had to call for Sam to drop everything and go running.

The following morning it was still raining and the waiting room smelt of damp clothes and central heating. It was a relief to be kept busy—at least that way she wouldn't have time to think. Even so, Kate's heart sank a little as she scanned the list.

'Looks like we could be in for another long day. Give me a couple of minutes to get my breath back, then you can send the first patient in,' she said as Lucy handed over the notes. 'By the way, I don't suppose those X-ray results arrived?'

'They certainly did.' Smiling, Lucy handed over a large envelope. 'There you go.'

'Well, thank heavens for that.' Kate glanced at the brief notes and gave a small sigh of relief. 'That's good news, anyway.' She smiled. 'Perhaps it's not going to be such a bad day after all.'

'I'd touch wood if I were you. I don't suppose you've heard from Dr Slater?'

'No.' Kate purposely kept her head lowered over the notes she was scribbling in her diary. 'But, then, I didn't expect to. He's probably busy. Heavens, is that the time? I'd better make a start.'

She wished Lucy hadn't mentioned Sam. She'd been doing her best not to think about him. Where was he? she wondered. What was he doing that was so important? When would he be back?

If nothing else, the past couple of days had given her the

briefest insight into what it would be like not to have him around, and she didn't like it.

So much had changed in what seemed like an extraordinarily short space of time. In the past few weeks the edges of her reasoning seemed to have become blurred. She enjoyed her work. Her life had been relatively uncomplicated—and then Sam had walked into it, turning everything upside down.

The empty consulting room was like a tiny oasis of peace in the untidy jumble of her thoughts. Shedding her coat, she checked her appearance in the mirror—fashionable trousers, ivory-coloured shirt and a loose-fitting jacket.

Seating herself at the desk, she made a phone call and some minutes later pressed the buzzer.

By mid-morning, she was almost beginning to regret her wish to be kept busy. It was market day and market day brought people into town, and most of them liked to kill two birds with one stone, collecting prescriptions or visiting the surgery at the same time.

Two and a half hours later she straightened, easing her aching shoulder muscles. Finishing a letter she was writing to a specialist at one of the mainland hospitals, she sealed the envelope and reached for the phone. She was still speaking when Jill tapped at the door and poked her head round. Kate beckoned her in.

'Yes, Geoff. No, I really appreciate it. I hate having to ask a favour but this patient has been getting steadily worse... You're a real friend.' She laughed.

From the door, Jill mouthed, 'I'll come back later.' But Kate motioned her to come in.

'I'll send you a report, then, and look forward to hearing from you soon. How's Angela? Oh, great. Give her my love. Bye.' Kate replaced the receiver.

'Sorry about that. I thought you'd finished.'

'Don't worry about it. I was just calling Geoff Seagrove.'

'The orthopaedics chappie?'

'Yes, that's right. I decided to try and pull a few strings. I know it's awful of me, but I want to get Mrs Crozier's hip operation done as soon as possible. She's in agony. Last time I saw her she said life wasn't worth living, and that's not like her. Anyway, that's my problem. What can I do for you?'

Jill frowned. 'A bit of sad news, I'm afraid, but I thought you'd want to know. I had a call from Mrs Matthews about half an hour ago.'

'Not Ed?'

Jill nodded. 'I'm afraid so. It seems she popped in this morning as usual, and found him still in bed. At first she thought he'd just overslept. Then she realised that he wasn't breathing. It looks as if he died in his sleep. She says the end must have been very peaceful.'

Kate swallowed hard. 'Poor Ed.'

'He was a nice old chap. Life wasn't exactly easy for him, was it?'

'No, I don't think it was, especially after his wife died.' Kate reached for a hanky and blew her nose. 'This is ridiculous. I should be used to this sort of thing by now.'

'*Do* you ever get used to it?'

'No, probably not. Oh, but didn't you say something about his daughter?'

Jill nodded. 'That's what makes it so sad. She didn't get here in time to see him. But at least he got to speak to her on the phone before he died, so you could say they were at least reconciled.' She sighed. 'Maybe the excitement was just too much for him.'

'I suspect he'd just had enough,' Kate said softly.

It wasn't the best of endings to the day, she thought as she made her way out to her car.

* * *

It was late when finally Kate was able to head for home. Early evening and it was already dark. The sky was clear and there was a distinct chill in the air.

She stirred restlessly. Suddenly the prospect of going back to the empty cottage seemed less than inviting.

Illogically, her spirits rose as she drove past Sam's place, perhaps Sam was back by now, until she discovered that it was still in darkness and there was no sign of his car. Disappointment knotted her throat as minutes later, having pulled up in her drive and switched off the engine, she climbed out and let herself into the cottage, switching on the lights.

She checked the answering machine. There were no messages. So where are you, Sam? What's keeping you? She batted the thought away. Some things it was better not to know.

She flipped the switch on the electric kettle, reached for the milk and absent-mindedly poured it into the teapot. What am I doing? she asked herself with a small sigh of disgust.

This is ridiculous, she thought crossly. All right, Sam is late—so what? She stifled a yawn as she popped bread into the toaster and hunted in the refrigerator for the remnants of a piece of cheese. 'So he needn't expect me to cover for him tomorrow if he doesn't turn up,' she muttered furiously under her breath as she rescued the smouldering toast. 'That's what.'

Carrying the improvised meal on a tray into the small sitting room, she made a perfunctory attempt at eating while she watched the day's news on television.

'Just the sort of cheerful stuff I need at the end of a long day.' She sighed, zapped the screen into darkness again and leaned her head back, briefly closing her eyes. Which was a mistake because her mind immediately, frustratingly, only conjured up images of Sam.

'Oh, what the heck. I need an early night anyway.'

Having showered and slipped into her nightie, she climbed into bed, sipping at a cup of hot cocoa. She willed the phone not to ring. The idea of having to get dressed again and turn out into the chilly night to answer an emergency call was almost too much to contemplate.

Reaching for her watch, she stared at the small dial. Ten o'clock. 'This is pathetic, Kate Dawson,' she muttered. 'When were you last in bed by ten o'clock, for heaven's sake?'

With a hint of defiance she switched off the light and pulled the covers over her head.

Suppose Sam doesn't come back, a tiny voice insisted, and was instantly banished. Sighing, she pushed the covers down and lay, staring up at the ceiling. Don't be ridiculous. Of course he's coming back. He has to. He hasn't said goodbye.

She sighed again. I'm not going to think about Sam. I *won't* think about Sam. What Sam does with his life is his own affair. She flinched at her use of the word and its obvious connotation. Glancing at the clock, she lay with her arm flung across her eyes. He's probably home in bed by now, and snoring his head off.

The sound of the phone shrilling by the side of her bed brought her gasping back to wakefulness. Kate lay for a few seconds, battling with a sense of disorientation as she tried to remember where she was.

Groaning, she reached for the bedside-light switch. Dragging a hand through her hair, she reached for the phone.

'H-hello?'

There was a moment's hesitation before a deep, male

voice spoke in her ear. 'This is Sam. I hope I didn't disturb you.'

More than he could possibly know, she thought wildly, staring at the alarm clock in disbelief. She must have fallen into a deep sleep that had lasted all of ten minutes!

'No...' She cleared her throat. 'Not at all.' Instinctively her hand drew the sheet higher before she chided herself for the gesture. It wasn't as if he could see her in the flimsy nightdress, was it?

He sounded tired. 'I thought I'd better let you know, I just got back. I've only just realised how late it is. You were probably asleep.'

'As a matter of fact I was...just catching up on some reading.' Mentally Kate crossed her fingers on the lie.

'In that case I'm glad I caught you. I just wanted to let you know that I'll be on call tonight, and to thank you for covering for me.'

'It's no problem.' She cleared her throat. 'H-how did your visit go?' Why am I asking? she thought wildly. I really don't want to know how he spent his time with another woman.

He gave a small laugh. 'The time went too fast.'

'I can imagine. You must have had a lot to talk about.'

'It was certainly good to catch up on all the news.'

Kate swallowed hard and with an effort managed to keep her voice even. 'I'm glad it all went well.'

'Anyway, I don't know about you, but I'm exhausted. I'll say goodnight, then, and thanks again. At least now you can stop worrying.'

'Goodnight.' Her voice sounded husky.

She replaced the receiver. Sam was home. Worried? Who was worried? With a sigh she switched out the light, relaxed and closed her eyes.

CHAPTER NINE

THE Hollisters were a young family, living on one of the new estates that had sprung up on the island in the past couple of years—Mum, Dad, two children and another baby on the way.

Kate knew them all through their various visits to the surgery for treatment for routine childhood ailments, vaccinations and antenatal clinics. She knew Debbie Hollister to be a sensible enough young woman, so if she phoned at seven in the morning, sounding fairly agitated, there was likely to be a very good reason.

The door of the neat, semi-detached house opened just as Kate reached it.

'Oh, Doctor, it's good of you to get here so quickly. I'm sorry to have to call you out. Come in.'

Kate brushed droplets of rain from her jacket. She smiled. 'I thought I'd do the visit before I start surgery, as it was on my way anyway. It's one of the children, is it?'

'That's right. It's young Hal. He's through here.' Debbie Hollister led the way into a neatly furnished sitting room, where her husband, Steve, was pacing the floor, nursing a flushed and tearful infant against his shoulder. 'We've hardly had a wink of sleep.'

Steve Hollister shot a look of relief in Kate's direction. 'Oh, are we glad to see you.'

'He's been crying nearly all night, Doctor. I thought it might be wind, or maybe he was cutting some more teeth, but I've had a look and I can't see any sign. I gave him a dose of Calpol a couple of hours ago.'

'Did it help?' Kate put her briefcase down.

'Not so that you'd notice. Not for long, anyway. He dozed off for about half an hour, then he woke again suddenly and he's been like this ever since.'

'Let's take a look at him.' Kate eased off her jacket and took the crying infant onto her knee. 'He's certainly not a very happy little chappie, is he?'

'I was going to bring him along to the surgery this morning, but we started getting really worried when he just wouldn't stop crying, and I'm sure he's got a temperature.'

'You did absolutely the right thing in calling me,' Kate smiled reassuringly. 'He certainly feels hot.' She reached for a thermometer, popping it into the child's armpit. 'Let's see how high it is. Meanwhile, I'll just take a quick look at you, shall I, young man?'

She made a careful examination for any swollen glands and managed, with difficulty, to peer down his throat.

'Hmm, that's slightly red, but it's certainly not infected.' She retrieved the thermometer and frowned. 'Yes, well, his temperature is certainly up. Has he been sick?' She reached into her briefcase for a stethoscope.

'No.'

'There's no sign of any rash. Let's have a listen to your chest, shall we? Yes, that's clear, too.' She looked at the baby's flushed cheeks. 'I think we'd better check your ears. We're running out of ideas here, young man. Yes, I know, you don't like this, do you?' With a slightly apologetic smile she produced an auroscope and proceeded to examine his ears, under protest.

'Ah, and there we have it. All right, little fellow, you can go back to your mum. I don't blame you for being fed up.' She looked at Debbie and smiled. 'He's got a nasty ear infection. It's probably been coming on for a couple of days. The left one is slightly pink, but the right one is quite badly inflamed.'

'Poor old Harry.' Debbie kissed her son.

'I'm afraid he's probably going to be a bit miserable for a couple of days. It's a good thing you called me. Ear infections can be nasty things—they're not something you should ignore, especially in a small child.'

Kate took out a prescription pad. 'I'll write him up for a course of antibiotics. It's in syrup form with a quite pleasant taste, so he probably won't object to taking it, but I'm afraid it will take about forty-eight hours before it really starts to take effect. In the meantime you can give him Calpol to ease the pain and bring down his temperature.'

'I'm so grateful.' Debbie followed Kate to the door. 'I was just about at my wits' end.'

'It's always a worry when a small child is ill. Hopefully, though, he'll soon be feeling better.'

Driving to the surgery as the first streaks of sunlight were creeping into the sky, Kate had time to appreciate not only the beauty of the scenery, with the gulls wheeling over the waterline in the cove below, but also the peace and tranquillity of a time of day when the island's roads were still relatively free from traffic.

At least arriving early at the surgery had its advantages, she thought as she dealt, uninterrupted, with a backlog of mail and an assortment of seemingly never-ending official forms still waiting to be filled in.

It came as something of a surprise when Jill popped her head round the door to say, 'Hello, you're bright and early today. Or did you forget to go home last night?'

Kate looked up, grinning. 'Nothing so noble. I got a call out to the Hollisters' baby at about seven o'clock. It hardly seemed worth going home, so I thought I'd catch up on a few of the things I seem to have been putting off lately.'

She leaned back, stretched her arms above her head and yawned. 'It looks as if it's going to be a nice day. I was wondering, as I drove here, how the happy couple are doing—lying in the sun, having a great time.'

'Sooner them than me.' Jill grinned. 'Some folk get a nice tan, I just end up looking like a boiled lobster. Mind you.' She gave an exaggerated sigh, 'I expect I could put up with a week in the Seychelles if I put my mind to it.'

'Couldn't we all?' Kate laughed. 'Ah, well, back to earth with a bump. I take it we have a waiting room full of patients?'

''Fraid so. Oh, by the way, Sue asked if you could see Mrs Pritchard some time this morning?'

'I expect so. Why, what's the problem?'

'I'm not sure. I gather Sue saw her yesterday. Mrs Pritchard wasn't feeling too well. She had brought along a urine specimen to be tested, just in case, and Sue advised her to pop in and see you today. I've got the notes here somewhere.' She riffled through a stack of papers. 'Ah, yes, here they are.' She handed over a sheet of paper.

Kate glanced at it. 'Mmm. Yes. Can we fit her in some time this morning?'

'As it happens we had a cancellation, so I've pencilled her in for ten o'clock.'

'Great. According to this she definitely has an infection, so the sooner we get her started on antibiotics the better.' She said casually, 'Is Dr Slater in yet?'

'Yes, he arrived just ahead of me. He went straight to his room. I expect he's got a bit of catching up to do.'

'I expect so.' Kate made a play of tidying her desk. 'Oh, I've signed these letters, by the way, so they can go in the post, and these are for typing.'

It was a typically busy morning. Most of her patients seemed to be suffering from heavy colds or self-inflicted backache, and she found herself wondering why they didn't simply stay at home and dose themselves with whatever favourite remedy suited them best, rather than coming to the surgery.

By the time she finally saw her last patient out and went gratefully in search of coffee, she took her own advice and was just swallowing a couple of aspirins when the door opened and Sam stood there.

He was wearing dark trousers and a sweater, and he looked tired. It needed an effort of will on her part not to go to him and put her arms around him. Instead, she reached for another cup, poured the coffee and handed it to him.

He grinned. 'You're a mind-reader. I really need this.'

'You look awful.'

'Thanks a lot.' His mouth twisted. 'I didn't expect to be quite so late getting back. I hope I didn't disturb you last night?'

Not nearly as much as he was disturbing her now. Kate ran a shaky hand through her hair, before turning to help herself to a biscuit—anything to keep herself occupied.

'Not at all. Like I said, I was catching up on some reading and lost track of the time.' She watched as he drank the scalding liquid gratefully.

'I'm sorry I had to ask you to cover for me, especially with Tim away.'

His height and presence in the small room were having a strange effect on her. Sam was standing only an arm's length away and she found herself wanting to reach out, to touch him, to draw him closer.

'Forget it.' She managed a smile as she refilled her own cup. 'As long as you don't plan on making a habit of it.'

His glittering gaze was brooding. 'Dare I hope you missed me, Kate?'

Her pulse rate accelerated dangerously. She chose deliberately to misunderstand. 'It might help if next time you don't choose to go in the middle of a chickenpox epidemic.'

'That wasn't quite what I had in mind,' he said huskily, moving closer, and she found herself gazing breathlessly at the firm line of his jaw, the sensual mouth and the blue eyes, which seemed to be having a strangely hypnotic effect, drawing her towards him.

The softness of his sweater brushed against her skin, sending dangerous signals to her brain.

'I—I have things to do.' She had to clear her throat. 'I shouldn't be here. I'll catch up with you later maybe.'

'Kate?'

She hesitated at the door.

'Is it too late to take you up on that offer of a meal?'

She swallowed hard and thought, You're not making this easy, Sam. Right now it would take very little to make me end up in your arms. But would that be wise?

She moistened her dry lips with her tongue. 'I can't make it tonight. I'm taking late surgery.'

'So why don't we say the day after tomorrow?'

Why, indeed? If she stopped to think about it she could probably come up with a whole lot of reasons. She met his gaze and swallowed hard.

'I'll have to shop. I'm afraid the cupboard is pretty bare.'

'No problem. I tell you what—I'll cook.'

A day off had its advantages unless you preferred not to be alone with your thoughts, and right now thinking was playing havoc with her nerves, Kate decided as she ran a hand through her hair in a small, nervous gesture.

For some crazy reason she felt like a schoolgirl on her

first date, except that there was nothing even remotely childlike about her feelings for Sam.

Having showered, washed her hair and brushed it until the honey-blonde waves shone, Kate went through the contents of her wardrobe, and felt the nervousness she had been fighting all day well up with new intensity.

Just because Sam was back it didn't mean he was here to stay, her inner voice warned her. She couldn't imagine what had possessed her to agree to have dinner with him, especially alone at his cottage, but it was too late to back out now.

She decided finally to wear plain but elegant black trousers, which draped softly against her hips, and a cream-coloured sweater. Gold clips in her ears and a simple gold chain at her throat added a touch of sparkle.

Slipping her feet into slender-heeled shoes, she took a deep breath before collecting from the kitchen her mobile phone and the bottle of red wine.

When she arrived at Sam's a few minutes later, he opened the door at the same instant that she reached it, almost as if he had been waiting for the sound of her car on the drive. She hesitated in the doorway.

'I hope I'm not too early. I brought this wine. I hope it's all right—' She broke off, aware of his penetrating gaze raking her slowly from head to toe, lingering with disturbing intensity on the curve of her breasts and the narrowness of her waist, emphasised by the trousers. Panic hit her. She stared down at herself, then at his own casual jeans and a sweatshirt and passed her tongue over her dry lips. 'I wasn't sure what to wear.'

'You look fine. Better than fine. You look beautiful,' Sam said softly. 'You'd better come in.' She slipped into the neatly furnished sitting room. 'Make yourself at home.

I just need to do a few domestic-type things in the kitchen. How do you like your steak, by the way?'

'As it comes. I really don't mind,' she called after him.

Listening to the sounds coming from the kitchen, Kate took advantage of the moment to study the room, her eye caught by the details, subtle changes he had made even in so short a time. Changes which stamped his own personality upon it—pictures on the walls, an arrangement of dried flowers in the open hearth, a lamp reflected in the polished surfaces. A faint breeze stirred the curtains at the open window.

'I'll be with you in a minute. Why don't you pour some drinks?'

'I'm on call, don't forget.' She raised her voice to remind him.

'I keep trying.'

She spun round to see him standing in the doorway. 'How about some orange juice?' He came towards her and she accepted the proffered glass, sipping at the contents.

'Mmm, nice. Can I do anything to help out there?'

Sam shook his head. 'I'm not the world's best cook but I think I can just about handle steak and a salad. Everything seems to be under control.'

Except my heart, she thought wildly. She could feel the pulse hammering in her throat as he looked at her. There was something disturbingly arousing about him as he stood there, the faded jeans hugging his hips, his eyes appearing a deeper blue than ever. His nearness was creating an intensity of sexual awareness that took her breath away.

Kate let her gaze fall warily. 'I feel guilty. I'm not used to being waited on.'

'Why not just relax and enjoy it?' Sam looked at her searchingly. 'Come here,' he said softly, holding his arms out to her. 'You look tired.'

'As bad as that?' she murmured, but she went anyway, allowing him to fold her in his arms, to soothe away the tensions of the day. It felt good, and right. Like...coming home.

'I'm not sure this is a good idea,' she murmured breathlessly, tilting her head back to look at him.

'I think it's a great idea.'

For an instant she felt him tense and then, suddenly, he bent his head and his mouth was making teasing advances against her lips, her throat, the lobes of her ears and back to her shamelessly unresisting mouth, claiming it with a determination that left them both breathless.

The effect was devastating. Without warning his palm slid round her waist, drawing her towards him. His mouth was warm and firm and she responded with a ferocity that matched his own, driven by a raw kind of hunger.

When, finally, he released her, it was to say huskily, 'I think we'd better eat, before I forget why you're here and things get well and truly out of hand.'

She whispered, 'Suddenly I'm not sure I'm very hungry.'

Sam brushed a hand against her cheek. 'Come on, we can't let my culinary efforts go to waste.' He bent his head to brush his lips against her mouth. 'We can talk later, Kate. I've no intention of rushing things, no matter how much I might be tempted.'

Kate had told herself she wouldn't be able to eat a thing, but when it came to it she found she was ravenous. Confronted by the steak and salad and crusty bread—accompanied by the wine—she ate enthusiastically.

In no time at all, it seemed, her plate was empty and she sat back, disconcerted to find Sam watching her with a gleam of amusement in his eyes.

'I must have been more hungry than I thought,' she confessed slightly shame-facedly.

Sam grinned. 'Don't apologise. I like to see someone who enjoys their food. Come on.' He rose to his feet. 'I'll make some coffee later since, I suppose, brandy is out of the question. Right now I think I just want to be with you,' he said huskily, drawing her to her feet, his gaze holding hers. His blue eyes searched her face intently as he touched her cheek. 'Why don't we leave all this and just go and relax?'

The effect of his touch was more potent than brandy could have ever been. She drew a shuddering breath as his hand moved to caress her breast, and gasped as the taut nipple flowered in instant response.

She tilted her head back to look at him, her fingers brushing gently against his lips. 'I forgot to ask. Did you manage to sort out the problem, whatever it was?'

He grinned as his mouth made a small foray against her lips. 'Problem? What problem would that be?'

'Sam!' Playfully she pushed him away. 'I'm talking about Marie-Laure.'

'Marie-Laure?' He frowned. 'Where does she come into this?

Kate sighed. 'I know she means a lot to you. She must, for you to drop everything and go running.' She tried to release herself from his grasp, but his hold merely tightened. 'It can't have been easy, leaving her behind when you came back to England. You must miss her.'

His dark brows drew together. He ran his fingers gently through her hair. 'Yes, of course I miss her. I miss a lot of things. We worked together for three years. You get to know a lot about someone in that time. But I promise you—' his warm breath was against her hair '—there's nothing for you to worry about. Right now the only thing I want to think about is us. You and me, Kate.'

A nerve pulsed in his jaw then he drew her slowly towards him. He groaned softly as his lips claimed her unresisting mouth and she responded with a ferocity driven by desperation and raw need. Sam raised his head briefly, breathing hard as he stroked her hair.

'I promised myself I wouldn't rush things, but I want you, Kate.'

'I know.' He kissed her again. She could feel the heat of his body through the fabric of his sweatshirt. His hands had long since dealt with the fastenings of her bra and were moving over her body, rousing her to a peak of desperation.

She closed her eyes, moaning softly as a whole gamut of emotions ran through her.

'I do want you, Kate. I need you.'

'I know.' She sighed fretfully. 'I didn't intend for this to happen...'

He raised his head to look down at her with glittering eyes. 'I know you've been hurt, my love. All I can tell you is that I'd never do anything to make you unhappy.'

'But I thought I loved Colin,' she said weakly. 'I thought he loved me.'

'I know.' Sam's hand under her chin forced her to look at him.

'But why does it always go wrong?'

'It doesn't, not always, Kate. You were unlucky. You couldn't have known what Colin was like until it was too late. You made the wrong choice. It happens. But that doesn't mean we don't get a second chance. That we can't fall in love again. It *can* work. You have to believe that. Trust me.'

He was right, she saw that now. She had tried to fight it, to tell herself that after Colin she would never take that kind of risk ever again. But it was no defence against this man. She did believe him. She *could* allow herself to fall in love again.

The shock of the admission made her senses reel.

'Perhaps you need a little more persuading.' He raised his head to look at her, desire still flaring in his eyes. 'You have to let go of the past, Kate,' he said softly. 'It's time to move on. Your parents made their own mistakes. You weren't responsible. You were unlucky. It's as simple as that. There's a whole new life out there, just waiting for you to grasp it.' He cupped her face in his hands, his thumbs grazing her cheek.

'I didn't intend rushing things,' he rasped. 'I'm not sure I can stick to that. I want you, Kate.'

She rocked on her feet, her senses still drugged as she looked at him. 'I seem to have wasted so much time.' She closed her eyes, moaning softly.

He drew a harsh breath as he looked at her for a long moment, then pulled her roughly towards him. 'Stay with me tonight, Kate.'

His hands were moving over her body, rousing her again.

'This shouldn't be happening. It's completely crazy.'

'I know,' he breathed as he unfastened the belt at her waist.

Her mobile phone rang. Involuntarily, she stiffened.

'Ignore it,' he grated.

'I can't, Sam. I did tell you I was on emergency call.' She detached herself slowly from his arms.

He cursed softly under his breath, grinning as she fumbled to restore her clothing to order before reaching for the phone.

'Yes, Dr Dawson speaking.' She reached up to press her fingers against Sam's marauding lips. 'Yes, and she's been sick? What about her temperature? Yes, that is high. Right, I'll be there in about fifteen minutes.'

She struggled to her feet, raking a hand through her hair, guessing how she must look. She felt as if she had been savaged! Her mouth still felt swollen, her hair was wildly dishevelled where his fingers had raked through it.

'I have to go, Sam.'

'I know.' His mouth curved in a wry response as he followed her to the door, helping her into her jacket, his hands tightening on her shoulders. 'Hurry back. I'll be waiting for you.'

'I may be late.'

'It doesn't matter.' He kissed her. 'Just be as quick as you can.'

In the event, another call meant that it was over an hour before Kate was finally able to head back to Sam's cottage, exhausted but happy.

The evening was pleasantly mild—a brief taste of an Indian summer before winter finally set in with a vengeance, she thought.

Pulling up in the drive, she smilingly reached for her briefcase. The curtains had been partially drawn, but through the gap she could see that the lights were on, welcoming and warm.

She hurried towards the door. She raised her hand to ring the bell, but as she did so the sight of an unfamiliar car parked beneath the tree caused her to halt, frowning.

It was a little late for visitors, surely? She hesitated, uncertain what to do. Should she make her presence known, or slip away and come back later when whoever it was had gone?

As she stepped back into the shadows, a movement inside the cottage drew her attention. She looked through the window into the softly lit sitting room, and saw Sam.

He wasn't alone. As she watched, a young woman moved towards him, a glass in her hand, and looked up at him. Through the open window, Kate could hear their voices clearly.

'I'm not going to let you get away so easily, Sam. You must know I've always wanted you. Why else do you think I'm here?' She reached up to run a hand through Sam's hair before his hand came down and they kissed, oblivious to the figure gazing in at the window.

A wave of nausea threatened to engulf Kate. She couldn't believe it was happening. Her worst nightmare was coming true. History was repeating itself. How could Sam let it happen, when little over an hour ago he had held her in his arms and asked her to trust him—had said that he loved her?

It had all been lies, she could see that now. It was Marie-Laure he loved. For Kate had no doubt that Marie-Laure was the girl in Sam's arms, the girl she had seen in the photograph on Sam's desk.

Tears welled up in her eyes as slowly, shocked, she backed away. How could she have been so naïve, ever have imagined that she really knew Sam?

He'd said he wanted her. She didn't doubt that. But he had never said he loved her. Love, it seemed, was reserved for the other woman in Sam's life.

CHAPTER TEN

THE weekend was like a bad dream for Kate, to be got through somehow, anyhow. For once it was a relief to be on emergency call. She deliberately kept busy in a desperate attempt to shut out thoughts of Sam and Marie-Laure together, but somehow, no matter how hard she tried, she still couldn't rid her mind of those unhappy images.

On Sunday she went for a long walk along the coast road. Overnight, it seemed, winter had finally arrived, and in the bay below a gale drove the sea in huge white-capped waves against the harbour wall. Frustrated, she returned to the cottage, drew the curtains, switched on the lamps and prayed that the phone wouldn't ring.

On Monday morning she woke with a splitting headache and to the horrifying realisation that she had overslept, and consequently she arrived at the surgery five minutes late, breathless, and having had no breakfast.

Any hopes she might have had of being able to avoid Sam were dashed as he appeared just as she was at the Reception desk, checking her diary and the already long list of patients.

For an instant their eyes met and she experienced a brief sense of shock. He looked tired. Worse than that, he looked as if he had hardly slept. Which, she told herself resignedly, might be true.

'I've signed a prescription for Mr Fuller. Tell him I've changed the medication for his bronchitis, will you?' she said to Lucy, before turning away deliberately to study her list of calls with an attention it didn't warrant.

'Kate, wait!' Sam's hand came down on her arm. 'I need to talk to you. Meet me after surgery, please.'

'I'm sorry,' she said flatly. 'I don't have time. In any case, I really don't think we have anything to say to each other.' She tried to sidestep him but he refused to let her pass, his face taut as he looked at her.

'I waited for you the other night. You didn't come back.'

Yes, I did, Sam, she thought. But you were too busy and you didn't see me. Impatiently she pushed a stray wisp of hair behind her ear. 'No, it was late by the time I'd finished the call and I was tired. Besides...' she reached for a bundle of mail from the desk '...you had a visitor. You were obviously busy. I decided not to intrude. Now, if you'll excuse me, I really am busy.'

She turned away. 'Lucy? I need Mrs Kingsley's notes. The results of her smear test are through and I need to see her. She's coming in tomorrow, I think.'

Lucy's glance flickered between the two of them. 'Right. I'll hunt them out and put them on your desk, shall I?'

'Thanks. I'll make a start, then. It would be nice to get away before lunchtime for once.' She started to make her way along the corridor. She hoped Sam would go away, leave her alone before she made a complete fool of herself by bursting into tears. But he followed, his expression grim.

'Kate, please, let's talk. I know you're upset, but at least let me explain. It isn't what you're thinking.'

'Sam, you don't know what I'm thinking,' she said. 'I don't want to discuss it. I made a mistake, that's all there is to it. At least I realised in time and I won't make the same mistake again. Let's leave it at that, shall we?' She gave him a remote smile and turned away.

'Kate, please—'

'Dr Slater, there's a call for you...' Lucy's voice broke into the tension between them.

Sam swore softly under his breath. 'Damn it, not now. Can't you take a message?'

'It's about the results of Mr Crawford's scan. You did say it was urgent. I thought you'd want to speak to them...'

Sam raked a hand through his hair. 'Kate, please, don't do this. *Talk* to me.'

But she was already walking away. If she talked to Sam it wouldn't end there, she knew that. She would end up in his arms. Right now her anger was the only defence she had against him, and she was clinging to it the way a drowning man clung to a raft.

Somehow she got through the morning. Seeing the last of her patients out, she returned to her room, checked her diary and then made her way to Reception.

'Right, that's me finished here.' Handing over the cards she glanced at her watch. 'With a bit of luck I might just manage to grab some lunch before I start my calls.'

Jill glanced anxiously out of the window. 'I don't like the look of the weather out there. That wind is definitely getting stronger. I wouldn't be surprised if it causes some damage.'

Kate smiled. 'Better go and batten down all the hatches, then. If the worst comes to the worst, perhaps everyone will stay at home.'

Jill gave a small hoot of laughter. 'We should be so lucky. You don't imagine a mere gale will keep the patients away?'

A door opened along the corridor and Sam emerged, grim-faced.

'Yes, well, I'd better get going. I'll see you later, all being well.' By the time Kate had reached her car and was fumbling to get the key in the lock, Sam was beside her.

She cursed as the key refused to turn. Sam's hand came

down over hers. 'Kate, don't go. We can't leave things like this. We have to talk.'

'There's nothing to say, Sam,' she reiterated flatly. From the moment he had walked into her life it had become full of complications, she realised that now. Her own emotions were so close to the surface that she wasn't sure she could trust herself to be near him without breaking down. She felt as if she were walking on quicksand. The more she struggled to break free, it seemed the deeper she was being sucked in.

'I promise you, it isn't the way you think.'

But the damage, as far as she was concerned, was already done. Sam had taken her to the brink, had even allowed her a glimpse of the exquisite pleasure his love-making could have held. But that was as far as his commitment went.

She forced herself to look at him. There was no mistaking the strain on his face and never before had she been so starkly aware of her own vulnerability.

With an effort she turned the key in the lock. 'It really doesn't matter, Sam.' She wrenched the car door open and climbed in.

'At least talk to me, Kate.'

She sighed and shook her head. 'I think it would be better if we kept to a strictly business relationship from now on. That way no one gets hurt. There won't be any misunderstandings.'

But it was already too late for that, she thought as she drove away. Trust me, he'd said, and she had done just that. She had let her guard down and he had betrayed her.

Back at the cottage she drank a cup of coffee and swallowed a couple of aspirins as she checked the messages on her answering-machine. One more call to add to the list—at this rate she might even make it home before dark. The only bright thought in an otherwise dismal day, Kate thought as she made her way carefully along the country lanes.

The force of the wind had, if anything, strengthened, bending the overhanging trees, and torrential rain served only to make things worse.

By mid-afternoon the temperature had plummeted by several degrees and she had to switch on the car heater.

Switching on the radio, she half listened to the latest local news bulletin. 'An accident has closed part of the coast road... Driving conditions made worse... Gale force winds expected to continue for some time...'

Minutes later Kate climbed out of the car, locked the door and stood for a few seconds, breathing hard as she made the trek across the farmyard. The door was opened by an anxious-looking woman of about sixty.

'Sorry it took me a while to get to you, Doris,' Kate apologised as she stepped breathlessly inside the big, stone-built house, brushing droplets of rain from her hair as she did so. 'I had a list of calls as long as your arm and this weather is making it a bit hard going.'

'And I'm afraid there's no sign of it letting up for a while, not according to the forecast. Come in, Doctor. I was just making a cup of tea. Would you like one?'

'I'd love to, Dot...' Kate glanced, frowning, at her watch '...but I'd better not.' She smiled ruefully. 'I may be needed back at the surgery. Anyway, you said your mother isn't feeling too well?'

'That's right. She's been a bit off colour for the past few days.'

'In what way?'

'Oh, it's all a bit vague. She says she has a headache. It seems to get worse as the day goes on. I've given her some aspirin but that doesn't seem to shift it.' Shedding her apron, Dot led the way upstairs. 'She was dozing a while ago. That's not like her either.'

'You should have called me before, Dot. You know I said I'd come any time you were worried.'

'Well, you know how it is. We don't like to bother you. I did tell Mum I'd ring the surgery, but you know what she's like. She can't abide not being able to get about, so when she decided to stay in bed I knew things weren't right.' She pushed open the door. 'Hello, Mum. Look who's come to see you. She's a bit deaf,' she said to Kate. 'So you'll need to shout a bit.'

'Hello, Mrs Banks. Doris tells me you're not feeling too well today.'

The occupant of the bed emerged from beneath a mound of covers and struggled to sit up.

Kate looked at the older woman and felt a tiny ripple of shock run through her. Florence Banks seemed smaller, more vulnerable than when she had last seen her. Always tall and surprisingly strong after an active life, Florence Banks had suddenly, overnight it seemed, become a tiny, frail old woman.

Kate put her briefcase on the floor. Sitting in the chair beside the bed, she gently reached out to hold one small, blue-veined hand, her fingers registering the sluggish pulse.

Dot raised her voice as she said, 'I told the doctor you've got a nasty headache, Mum.'

'Aye.' Florence raised one frail hand, pressing it shakily to her forehead as she looked in Kate's direction.

Kate noted that the woman looked flushed. 'How long have you had the headache, Florence?'

She looked at her daughter and Dot nodded. 'About a week.'

'Is it there all the time?'

'Yes, I think so. It gets worse as the day goes on.'

Kate nodded. 'I just want to check your throat and glands.' She made a quick but thorough examination, pressing her fingers gently in the process against the woman's cheekbones and above her eyes. 'Does that hurt?'

'No.'

Kate smiled. 'Have you been feeling dizzy at all?'

'Aye, a bit.'

'Actually, now that you mention it, she had quite a nasty turn a couple of days ago. Nearly fell over. It was lucky I happened to be there at the time, wasn't it, Mum?'

'I don't want any fuss, now.' Florence flapped her hands, warding off her daughter. 'I told you, I didn't want you bothering the doctor.'

'It's no trouble at all, Mrs Banks.' Kate smiled. 'Now that I'm here I may as well check you over properly.' Uncoiling her stethoscope, she listened to her patient's chest. 'Well, that sounds fine. I'll just take a look at your ears. Ah.' She straightened up. 'There's the problem. Have you been feeling sick?'

'Well, now that you mention it...'

Kate smiled. 'And when you feel dizzy, do you fall to one particular side?'

'What is it, Doctor?' Dot Banks looked anxious.

Kate dropped the stethoscope into her briefcase and reached for her prescription pad. 'Your mother has labyrinthitis.' She raised her voice slightly. 'You have an inner ear infection, Mrs Banks. It's caused by a viral infection. It affects the semicircular canals of the ear. That's what is making you feel dizzy.'

'Can you do anything about it?' Dot said.

'Yes. I'll give you a prescription for some antibiotics to get rid of the infection. I'm sure they'll do the trick. Hopefully, in a couple of days, you'll be feeling a lot better,

Florence. Until then I suggest you rest in bed until the dizziness subsides.'

Kate wrote out the prescription, handing it to Dot. 'I wouldn't worry too much about her loss of appetite,' she said as they moved away from the bed. 'Just see that she drinks plenty of fluids. If you're at all worried, give me a call.'

It was almost dark when she returned to the practice, parked her car and ran through the gusting wind into the surgery. A peep into the crowded waiting room sent her hurrying through to Reception.

'What on earth happened?' She looked pointedly at her watch. 'It's like rush hour at Waterloo station out there. Where's Sam, for heaven's sake? Some of those patients are his.'

'I'm sorry. I don't know. He left just after lunch to do his visits. I think he was heading out toward Banford Point. We haven't heard from him since.'

The phone rang. Frowning, Lucy reached for it, cupping her hand over the receiver. 'He's probably just been delayed.'

'I wasn't sure I'd get here myself,' Jill said as she directed the next patient to the treatment room. 'This storm is causing all sorts of problems. Some of the roads are blocked by floods, and I heard something on the local radio about an accident on the coast road. It sounded pretty bad.'

Kate swallowed hard on the sudden dryness in her throat. 'I'd have thought Sam would use his mobile to call in if there was a problem.'

The phone began to ring in the office. Jill went to answer it, taking a pen and her notepad with her.

'Perhaps he can't use the mobile,' Lucy said. 'Reception may be bad. But I'm sure he's all right.'

With an effort, Kate managed a smile. 'Yes, I'm sure he

is. He probably just got sidetracked.' So why wasn't she convinced? 'Anyway, he wouldn't come along the coast road, would he?'

'He may not have had any choice. Some of the minor roads are closed. One of the patients said there was some bad flooding just out of town.'

'Sam's on the phone,' Jill interjected quietly as she came through from the office. She looked at Kate. 'He asked to speak to you.'

Relief swamped through Kate as she hurried into the office and reached for the phone, annoyed with herself now for having let her imagination run away with her.

'Sam, have you any idea what time it is? Things are going crazy here. Where are you, for heaven's sake?'

'Kate, I'm sorry it's taken so long to get through to you.' His voice was deep and gratifyingly strong. 'Look, something's cropped up. I'm afraid I'm not going to make it back in time for evening surgery. Can you cover for me, or see if any of the patients will be willing to rearrange their appointments? There's been an accident on the coast road.'

'Yes, Jill heard the news on the local radio.' She hesitated. 'Sam, are you all right?'

'Things are a bit of a mess here. I have to stay and do what I can to help. The emergency services are on the scene, but there are a couple of people trapped in their cars. It may take some time to get them out. I don't hold out too much hope for one of them.'

She heard muffled sounds in the background.

'Kate, I can't talk to you now. I have to go. I'll see you later.' He said something else, something which sounded amazingly like 'my darling.' But it couldn't possibly have been, she knew that. Then the line went dead.

Kate felt her stomach tighten. Only now, as she stared

at the receiver, did she realise that Sam hadn't actually answered her question when she'd asked if he was all right.

'Is everything all right, Kate?'

She turned slowly to find Jill and Lucy standing in the doorway.

Kate moistened her dry lips with her tongue. 'There's been an accident. It sounds pretty bad. Sam says there are a few serious injuries and a couple of people are trapped. He's helping out.'

Panic surged through her, flaring out of control. Why hadn't he answered her? Suddenly she knew that something was very wrong. Please, God, don't let Sam be hurt.

'I'm going out there.' She was already heading for the door.

Jill said anxiously, 'Is that wise?'

'I don't know. Maybe not, but I can't just sit here and wait. He may need help.' She hesitated. 'Will you…?'

'Don't worry. I'll explain things to the patients and see if I can get them to come back tomorrow.'

Kate nodded, only half listening as she grabbed her jacket and briefcase and ran to the car.

The drive to the site of the accident seemed to take for ever. The wind was, if anything, blowing even more strongly. The roads were littered by fallen branches and debris. Some of the smaller lanes were flooded.

The scene, when she arrived, was almost eerie. Hastily rigged lights were trained on the tangle of wreckage which had once been several cars.

One vehicle hung precariously over the grass-covered slope of the coastal path. Far below, Kate could hear the sound of the sea as the oncoming tide drove it relentlessly over the shingle and up against the sea wall.

It was like the worst kind of nightmare and somewhere,

in the middle of all that, was Sam. The thought filled her with dread.

Parking the car on the muddy verge, Kate grabbed her briefcase and the waterproof jacket she always kept in the car. She gasped as she opened the door, swaying slightly as the full force of the wind hit her.

'Sorry, miss.' The local police sergeant came towards her. I'm afraid you can't go any further. Oh…it's you, Doctor. I didn't recognise you for a minute.'

With an effort, Kate managed a slight smile. 'I'm not surprised. I heard about the accident, but I had no idea… My colleague, Dr Slater, is here already.' She looked at him. 'What happened, Bill? How…how bad is it?'

'It's a real mess.' Bill Stone shook his head. 'The gale brought a couple of trees down. One landed across the road and, of course, in the dark the drivers didn't see it. One car hit it. The rest just kept coming.'

He stepped aside as a couple of members of the fire crew struggled over the debris towards the wreckage.

'It couldn't have happened at a worse time. People heading home from work, most of them trying to avoid the floods, so they came this way. I've never seen anything quite like it and I've seen a few in my time. I'm glad you're here. We need all the help we can get.'

'How many casualties?' Kate asked as she began to pick her way precariously over pieces of twisted metal and fallen branches.

The wind whipped at her hair and she paused, gasping painfully for breath, trying to shield her face against the force of the wind. She pushed the stray wisps back, gritting her teeth as the icy rain lashed in from the sea. Bill Stone's hand came under her arm, supporting her, and she was grateful.

'Five, so far,' he said. 'A couple were minor injuries—

one of those was a kiddy, thank God. His mum had a sprained wrist and a few cuts from flying glass, but they were lucky. One had serious head injuries.'

He motioned towards a car lying on its side in the ditch. 'I'm not sure he'll make it. One dead—the rest, I don't know.' His mouth twisted. 'We haven't been able to get one of the drivers out of his car yet. He's not looking too good.'

As he spoke an ambulance set off, its siren wailing, into the night. 'We've managed to shift most of the vehicles, but the fire chaps are going to have to cut the tree into sections to shift if from across the road before we can get to the injured man.'

Kate's fingers clenched into fists and she swallowed hard. 'What about Dr Slater? I can't see him. Was he actually involved in the crash?'

'I gather he was one of the tail-enders. Damn bad luck. There was no way he could have avoided it. I haven't seen him, but one of the paramedics said he had head and shoulder injuries. He tried to persuade him to go to hospital with the other casualties but he insisted on staying with the young chap trapped in the car.'

Bill shook his head. 'He's got more guts than I have. Some of those other trees are looking decidedly dodgy. If another comes down on top of this lot we're in real trouble.'

Kate felt sick. 'I have to find him. He'll need some help.'

'I'm really not sure that's a good idea...'

'I brought some extra medical supplies with me. He may need them.'

'It's a hell of a risk. Like I said, those trees...'

She smiled wryly. 'Then the sooner I get in there and start helping the better, don't you think?'

'I'll come with you.'

'No, better not. We'll probably need all the space we can get. But thanks for the offer anyway.'

Slowly, carefully, she managed to manoeuvre her way over the fallen tree and the twisted metal debris. It was raining more heavily now as, shining the torch ahead of her, she made her way along the length of the tree, peering under the branches, all the time conscious of the acrid smell of leaking petrol.

It was even worse than she had dared imagine. She gasped with horror at the sight of a small car wedged solidly beneath the fallen tree. A large branch had smashed through the windscreen and was wedged inside the car. The front passenger seat was crushed almost beyond recognition.

Her foot slipped on wet leaves. Gasping, she flung out a hand to save herself, sending the beam of the torchlight through the window. Her heart gave a momentary lurch as she saw Sam.

He had eased himself forward from the back seat, over the gear lever, and was supporting the injured man's head. His face looked grey and haggard and he was bleeding from a head wound.

He drew a ragged breath as he looked at her for one long, disbelieving moment, and she told herself she must have imagined the flicker of relief she had seen on his face as he rasped, 'Are you crazy? What the hell are you doing here? Get out of here, Kate—*now*.'

She edged closer, glancing up briefly at the creaking, overhanging branch of a swaying tree. Please, don't fall now, she prayed silently. Carefully, she tugged fragments of broken glass out of the window. 'I guessed you'd probably need some help.'

'Well, I don't.'

'I'm not going to argue with you, Sam.' She saw the thin

trickle of blood seeping slowly from the wound at his temple. Her eyes blurred with sudden tears. She blinked them away, knowing this wasn't a good time to get emotional.

Reaching into her pocket for a handkerchief, she pressed it gently to the wound.

'Hang on in there, Sam. They'll soon have you out.' She had to raise her voice to make herself heard above the noise. 'They're trying to cut away the metal but they have to shift part of the tree as well.'

She glanced at him and felt her heart give an extra thud as he closed his eyes.

'Sam! Sam, don't you dare go to sleep.'

His eyelids flickered open and he gave a small wry smile. 'It's all right, Kate. I'm still with you.'

And I want you to stay that way, she thought. Whatever else happens, Sam, you've got to be all right. That's all that matters.

She eased herself closer, tugging gently at the buckled door on the driver's side of the car so that she could see the injured man.

'How is he?'

'I'm not sure. He's taken a pretty hard knock on the head.' The response was terse. 'He's still unconscious. He's got head and neck injuries. I'm afraid there may be spinal involvement—that's why I don't want to move him.'

'Has he regained consciousness at all?'

'Briefly. I've given him a shot of painkiller. I don't know how long it will be before the effect wears off. I seem to have lost track of the time. Where the hell is that rescue team?'

'They're all out there, Sam. Just hang on. It won't be much longer.'

'I'm not worried for myself, I just think he needs to be in hospital.'

'If I can get closer perhaps I can take a look at him.'

'I just wish you'd get the hell out of here, Kate,' Sam's voice rasped.

'I'm not leaving, Sam, so save your breath.' She worked her way closer, her hand gently easing open the injured man's shirt as she felt for a heartbeat. He groaned softly. 'It's all right. I'm a doctor. Try not to move. We're soon going to get you out of here.' Please, God, she thought.

For the first time she was able to see the man's features clearly. 'He can't be more than twenty,' she murmured softly. His short, dark hair was matted with blood, his breathing shallow.

'Sam, let me take over from you in there. I can support his head and neck while you move.'

He shook his head. 'I don't want to risk moving him, not without knowing the full extent of his injuries. Where the hell is that stretcher?'

'It'll be here, Sam.' She glanced at his pale features. 'What about you? You're hurt.'

'I'm fine.' He used his shoulder to wipe away a trickle of blood. 'It's worse than it looks.'

She frowned. 'Well, if you can't come out, Sam, I'm coming in.'

'There's no need. There's no room,' he rasped.

'Well, then, we'll *make* room. It may have escaped your notice, Sam, but I'm getting wet through out here.'

For the first time his mouth twisted in a semblance of a smile. 'You don't give up easily, do you, Dr Dawson?'

She eased herself carefully into the rear seat and looked at him, feeling the tears well up. His eyes looked like dark bruises in the paleness of his features. 'You'd better believe it.' She swallowed hard on the lump in her throat. 'I can't let you out of my sight for five minutes, can I, without you going off and doing something crazy?'

His free hand reached out, his fingers twining with hers as he pulled her towards him. Instinctively, she squeezed his hand. 'Are you suggesting that I need looking after?' The words came slowly, almost in a whisper.

But wasn't that Marie-Laure's job? She closed her eyes and blinked hard, before giving a short laugh. 'That sounds like a full-time job to me.'

'We're not in any hurry, Kate. We've got all the time in the world.'

Or maybe no time at all. A bubble of panic welled up, then she screamed as she heard an ominous cracking sound. Suddenly falling branches and debris were raining down on the car. Oh, God, no, not now. She became aware of Sam's arm, thrown around her, protecting her as he cradled her head against the taut muscles of his chest.

He released a pent-up breath. 'It's all right, Kate.'

Terror gave an added edge to her voice as she tilted her head to look at him. 'No matter what happens, I want you to know that I love you, Sam. You were right, we do need to talk.'

'Oh God…'

She froze. 'Sam, what…?' In horrified silence she followed his gaze, felt the car sway slightly, then gave a tiny sob. 'It's all right. They're here. Everything's going to be all right. They'll have you out in a few minutes.'

She was vaguely aware of figures moving around the car.

'OK, Doc, we'll have you out of there in a couple of minutes now. Just hang on.' Simon Durrant, one of the paramedics, peered in at the shattered window. 'They've managed to clear the main branch. A few minutes more and we'll have this young chap on his way to hospital.'

Kate straightened up. Moments later she was out of the car, vaguely aware that she was shivering violently.

Beside her, Sam was on his feet, swaying, rubbing at his arm to restore the circulation. His features looked haggard.

Kate sighed, suddenly very weary. Her head was pounding. Her mind was exhausted, shattered by the fear that she might have lost Sam—except that he wasn't hers to lose, and never would be.

'We'll soon have you in the ambulance, sir. Best get that head of yours seen to.'

'I'll be fine,' Sam grated. 'It's a cut, that's all.'

The paramedic hovered. 'It might be best, just as a precaution. You never know with head wounds...'

Kate felt the muscles in Sam's arm tense. She said quickly, 'It's all right. I'm a doctor. I'll take him home and give him a check over, and if I think he needs to go to hospital I'll make sure he gets there.'

'Well, if you're sure?'

She nodded, taking Sam's arm, looking up at him. 'Come on, Sam, let's go home, shall we? You've done all you can here.'

'I'm *not* going to the hospital.'

She looked at him, and with an effort managed to give a slight smile. 'Now who's being stubborn?'

The drive back to her cottage seemed to take for ever. He sat slumped in his seat, saying nothing. She could feel the tension in him.

Switching off the ignition, she tried to summon the energy to move, to get out of the car. Sam sat beside her, making no attempt to do so.

'Come on,' she said. 'I think we both need some coffee.'

He drew a breath and turned his head to look at her. 'It's late.'

'I know, but I need to unwind.' She fumbled with her keys. 'I don't know about you, but I feel as if I'm still running on pure adrenalin.'

He followed her into the sitting room and stood with his hands in his pockets. She poured two large brandies. She proffered one glass and he looked at it, his mouth twisting. 'Hmm, strange coffee.'

'I don't know about you, Sam, but I need something a little stronger. I'll make the coffee later.' She looked at him as she sipped at her drink, and thought, Right now, what I need is to be in your arms.

'You'd better let me take a look at that cut,' she said aloud. That was a mistake—it meant she had to move closer. Her hand reached up and she was surprised to find that it was shaking. 'You're lucky, I think you'll get away without needing to have it stitched. I'll clean it up for you.' Suddenly her voice had an edge to it. She was feeling angry without really knowing why. She said briskly, 'How do you feel?'

'As if someone ran over me with a steamroller.'

'Well, what do you expect, if you will insist on playing the hero?' she snapped ungraciously. 'You were damn lucky, Sam. You do realise what might have happened...?' She broke off, suddenly shaking violently, only now beginning to realise the full enormity of it all, how close she had come to losing him.

Taking several deep breaths, she half turned away, only to feel Sam's hands on her shoulders, preventing her.

'Kate, what's wrong?'

She couldn't believe he was asking the question. She looked up, her face taut with strain, to find him watching her, his lips set in a hard, fierce line.

'Wrong? Nothing's wrong.' She swallowed hard, blinking away the tears that suddenly threatened to well up. 'Sam, don't you think I should call Marie-Laure?'

His dark brows drew together as he looked at her. 'Do you *want* to call her?'

'No, of course *I* don't. But she may have heard about the accident. She'll be worried sick, Sam. She'll want to be here with you.'

His own breathing was ragged as he held her, his hand cupping her chin, forcing her to look into his compelling, blue eyes. 'Kate, I've no reason to ring Marie-Laure. I know what you've been thinking, but you were wrong. It's you I need, Kate. You I want.' His face was gaunt as she stared up at him. Then, with a sob, she went into the safe refuge of his arms.

'Oh, Sam, I thought I'd lost you.'

He was speaking softly as he held her, his own throat tightening in painful spasms. 'It's all right. Everything's going to be all right,' his voice rasped.

'You could have been killed.' Her voice was muffled as he held her close.

'Hush!' His fingers brushed against her mouth, silencing the words, then, before she knew what was happening, his mouth came down on hers, gentle at first, then relentless, firm, demanding.

They clung together, Kate offering no resistance as his hands moved over her body. He raised his head briefly to look down at her. 'I do need you, Kate,' he groaned softly, claiming her mouth again with a fierce possession that left them both breathless.

She responded with a fervour that matched his own, filled with a desperate need to be part of him, to hold him and keep him safe.

'I love you,' he rasped.

'I love you, too,' she said brokenly.

Sam gazed wonderingly into her eyes, then, almost hesitantly, he drew her within the circle of his arms again.

'I thought I was dreaming when you suddenly appeared

out there. I'd been thinking about you, thinking that it had all been such a waste—'

'Don't, Sam.' Gently she pressed her fingers against his mouth, smoothed the damp hair from his forehead. 'I've been such a fool. I can see that now.' She had to force herself to speak through the tightness in her throat. 'When my marriage to Colin went so badly wrong...I told myself I'd never let myself be hurt that way again, that I'd never allow myself to feel this way about anyone...' Her voice broke. 'I realise that you love Marie-Laure, that she'll always be part of your life...'

A groan rose in his throat as he silenced her with a hungry kiss before raising his head to look at her.

'Kate, you're wrong. I know what you saw...what you think...but it wasn't the way you think. Yes, Marie-Laure means a lot to me. She was there for me at a time when I desperately needed a friend. But that's all there is between us—friendship. That's all there will ever be.'

She stared at him, wanting to believe him, but fear gave an edge to her voice. 'But...I heard her say...that she had always wanted you, that she wasn't going to let you get away so easily...'

'I know what you heard, Kate, but it wasn't the way it sounds—you have to believe that.' He looked down at her, his thumb gently stroking her cheek. 'There's only one special lady in my life, Kate, and that's you.'

'But...'

He frowned. 'Marie-Laure has been given funding to set up a second clinic. She was offered the job of heading the new team herself but decided she wants to stay at Ramindi.' He broke off to look at her, his hand brushing her cheek. 'She wanted to meet me to ask me if I would consider taking the job.'

'Oh, Sam...'

His mouth twisted in a smile as he looked at her. 'We'd worked together for nearly three years. She knew I had the necessary qualifications. I suppose I was an obvious first choice for the job.'

Kate drew a deep breath. 'I saw you kiss her.'

He frowned. 'I kissed a good friend, Kate. We were saying goodbye. That was what you saw. Marie-Laure flew back to Africa last night.'

'Poor Sam,' she murmured. 'And I didn't give you a chance to explain. I'm so sorry.'

'And so you should be, woman.' He made a soft growling noise as he caught her hand, imprisoning it in his. 'Do you have any idea of the kind of hell I've been going through this past couple of days? And then, on top of it all, this had to happen.' He brushed a hand gingerly against the wound on his forehead. 'It hasn't been a good time for me, Kate.' He bent his head to brush his lips against hers and looked at her, his eyes glittering. 'I think I'm entitled to a little sympathy, don't you?'

Kate raised herself to kiss his nose. 'I'll have to think about it. Some people will go to extraordinary lengths to get a bit of attention, Dr Slater.' She tilted her head back and saw his eyes narrow.

'There's only one person whose attention I need, Kate. Only one person I want in my life, and that's you.'

'So you don't have any doubts—about going back to Ramindi?' Kate frowned. 'You said you might go back.'

He kissed her again and this time it was more demanding. '*You* said I might go back, Kate. *I* said there would always be work to do out there, but there are other people just as capable as I am. Everything I want is right here,' he said huskily. 'Just as long as you're sure...'

She silenced him with a kiss, brushing her lips against his mouth. 'You were right, Sam. Colin was a mistake, but it won't happen again. This time I know it's right.' She tilted her head back to look at him, and smiled. 'I'm just about to take that leap in the dark, Sam, and you'd jolly well better be there to catch me.'

He looked down at her and drew her into his arms. 'I'm here, Kate. I'll always be here for you. For as long as you need me.'

She snuggled into his warm embrace. 'That's going to be for an awfully long time, Sam—a lifetime.'

'And it all starts here,' he murmured softly, before he kissed her again.

MILLS & BOON®
Makes any time special™

Mills & Boon publish 29 new titles every month. Select from...

Modern Romance™   Tender Romance™

Sensual Romance™

Medical Romance™   Historical Romance™

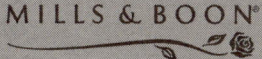

Medical Romance™

A MOTHER BY NATURE *by Caroline Anderson*
Audley Memorial Hospital

Adam Bradbury is a gifted paediatrician and a devoted father. But he is sure that his inability to have children of his own will push any woman away. But Anna knows that Adam is wrong and she is determined to prove it…

HEART'S COMMAND *by Meredith Webber*

Major Harry Graham had been drafted in to save the outback town of Murrawarra from torrential flood water but he hadn't bargained on Dr Kirsten McPherson's refusal to be evacuated…

A VERY SPECIAL CHILD *by Jennifer Taylor*
Dalverston General Hospital

Nurse Laura Grady knew that her special needs son, Robbie, would always be the centre of her life. Could paediatric registrar Mark Dawson persuade her that he wanted both of them to be the centre of his?

On sale 2nd February 2001

Available at most branches of WH Smith, Tesco, Martins, Borders, Easons, Volume One/James Thin and most good paperback bookshops

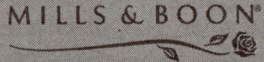

Medical Romance™

THE ELUSIVE DOCTOR by *Abigail Gordon*

Ambitious Dr Nina Lombard did not want to be in the quaint village of Stepping Dearsley! But now that she was working for Dr Robert Carslake, Nina found that she had a reason to stay...

A SURGEON'S REPUTATION by *Lucy Clark*

Dr James Crosby has made his attraction clear to Dr Holly Mayberry but something from his past is holding him back. When James's reputation is put on the line Holly knows she has a chance to win his trust and his heart...

DELIVERING LOVE by *Fiona McArthur*

New Author

Poppy McCrae has always used complementary therapies in her work as a midwife. Paediatrician Jake Sheppard thoroughly disapproves of her methods. Can Poppy persuade Jake to accept her and her beliefs?

On sale 2nd February 2001

Available at most branches of WH Smith, Tesco, Martins, Borders, Easons, Volume One/James Thin and most good paperback bookshops

MILLS & BOON

THIS TIME...
MARRIAGE

Three brides get the chance to make it This Time... Forever.

**Great value—
3 compelling novels in 1.**

Available from 2nd February 2001

books and a surprise gift!

We would like to take this opportunity to thank you for reading this Mills & Boon® book by offering you the chance to take FOUR more specially selected titles from the Medical Romance™ series absolutely FREE! We're also making this offer to introduce you to the benefits of the Reader Service™—

- ★ FREE home delivery
- ★ FREE gifts and competitions
- ★ FREE monthly Newsletter
- ★ Exclusive Reader Service discounts
- ★ Books available before they're in the shops

Accepting these FREE books and gift places you under no obligation to buy, you may cancel at any time, even after receiving your free shipment. Simply complete your details below and return the entire page to the address below. *You don't even need a stamp!*

YES! Please send me 4 free Medical Romance books and a surprise gift. I understand that unless you hear from me, I will receive 6 superb new titles every month for just £2.40 each, postage and packing free. I am under no obligation to purchase any books and may cancel my subscription at any time. The free books and gift will be mine to keep in any case.

M1ZEA

Ms/Mrs/Miss/Mr ....Initials................................
BLOCK CAPITALS PLEASE

Surname ....

Address ....

....

....Postcode....................................

Send this whole page to:
UK: FREEPOST CN81, Croydon, CR9 3WZ
EIRE: PO Box 4546, Kilcock, County Kildare (stamp required)

Offer valid in UK and Eire only and not available to current Reader Service subscribers to this series. We reserve the right to refuse an application and applicants must be aged 18 years or over. Only one application per household. Terms and prices subject to change without notice. Offer expires 31st July 2001. As a result of this application, you may receive further offers from Harlequin Mills & Boon and other carefully selected companies. If you would prefer not to share in this opportunity please write to The Data Manager at the address above.

Mills & Boon® is a registered trademark owned by Harlequin Mills & Boon Limited.
Medical Romance™ is being used as a trademark.